THE JUNIOR

Anna Sanclement

THE JUNIOR

Published in USA 2009
Softcover edition 2009

Published by Gravitron
Lulu/Anna Sanclement

This is a work of fiction. Names, characters, places and incidents either are
the product of the author's imagination or are used fictitiously.
Any resemblance to actual persons, living or dead, events,
or locales is entirely confidential.

Book design by Anna sanclement

ISBN 978-0-578-00852-3

Printed in the United States of America

www.lulu.com

To my family who always supports me
even when they thought I couldn't write.
Thanks!

One

As I mopped the coffee stained floor, an annoying tap on my shoulder startled me. I turned to find Elsie, the Café's Lead Team Member, staring at me and scowling.

"Did I not show you a hundred times how to mop?" she scolded me, yanking the mop from my hand. "See, this is how you hold it, making a forty-five degree angle with the floor as you swoop it. Didn't they teach you anything in training?"

She shoved the mop back at me, and put her hands on her waist. "Let's see you do it."

I stared at her.

"Well, c'mon, what are you waiting for? Do it like I showed you."

I dunked the mop into the bucket, splashing brown soapy water all around, then I lifted it up without wringing it and proceeded to mop all over Elsie's shoes. I went back and forth about 4 times, until I was sure her shoes were nice and soaked. Smiling, I handed the mop back to her.

"Is this better?"

The look on her face was worth a million bucks. I took my apron off, hung it on the nearest chair and walked out of the Readingworld Books Café.

I open my eyes and shiver. Scratching out the circle I have drawn around the Readingworld Books Café Worker job ad on the classifieds, I sigh heavily. Either I need to get some sleep, or I'm completely out of my mind. I don't know what possessed me to consider another job there, as if the experience four years ago wasn't bad enough. At least back then I was a college student; I think now, at twenty-seven and with a college degree, I should aspire for something more. Still, I'm growing desperate. I have sent at least 100 resumes in the last 3 months and I haven't found a job yet. I've been to countless painful interviews and no one has called me back.

I finally graduated from college last May - after changing majors five times - and now that I'm out in the real world, my optimism is really shrinking. I feel like any chances for finding my dream job are getting slimmer by the day. Feeling mentally exhausted, I put down the paper and go straight to bed.

The loud ringing of the telephone wakes me up and I'm surprised to see the daylight through the window; I look at my clock by the nightstand: 10:30 a.m. Realizing it could be an employer prospect, I clear my throat and say hello to my cat a couple of times, making sure I don't sound like a frog.

"Hello?" I say as clearly as possible, wishing I had looked at the caller ID before answering, but I'm still half asleep and can't fully think yet.

"You're still sleeping?"

I'm relieved to hear Courtney's voice on the other end. "Give me a break, I didn't get to bed until passed 3 am!"

"Where did you go and how come I wasn't invited?" She whines.

"To my couch, I was circling the classifieds all night." I sigh. "Trust me, you didn't miss much..."

She agrees. "Listen, what are you doing later? I need to talk to you, I've got some fantastic news!"

"I'll just be here circling more ads, and waiting for phone calls." I say sarcastically, and then add, "What news? Just tell me over the phone."

"No. I've got to tell you this face to face! I get off work at five thirty, so meet me at Nellys at say... around six?"

I spend the next hours scoping the classifieds, printing out cover letters and copies of my resume. By the time I finish I realize I could apply for jobs as a secretary and paper clerk in addition to a graphic designer. I leave the house at five, and drive to Kinko's to fax my resume arsenal, leaving the guy behind the counter amazed at the amount of pages I send out. He actually tells me that they are hiring, and asks for a copy of my resume. It's very tempting, considering my luck with job hunting, but the thought of working somewhere that's open twenty four hours a day is kind of scary. After I put all the resumes in the mail I make my way down to Las Olas, the area near downtown Fort Lauderdale, where Nellys is. I find a parking space very close, managing to get there just after six.

Since Courtney isn't here yet, I get us a table on the outside terrace, and order our drinks.

"Hey!" I hear Courtney's voice, and I look up to see her making her way to the table. "Sorry, I'm late, traffic was ridiculous, been here long?"

"just a few minutes. I got you your usual" I point to the Vodka Tonic in front of her.

"Perfect. How I needed this!" She takes a long sip of her drink.

"So, what's this great news you have, Pablo proposed or something?"

"Pablo's history, girlfriend." She rolls her eyes. "He was an idiot." Courtney hasn't ever had a relationship longer than a month. According to her, she's sampling every type of guy (And I mean every single type) before she decides which type she likes, and when she finds it, she'll start hunting for a guy within that type. That's a great plan, if you want to dedicate half your life to it. But that's Courtney; for now. She'll probably change her strategy when she decides she wants a wedding before she's forty. I guess at twenty-five, she still has time.

She takes another sip of her drink and sits up, her face brightens with a big smile.

"You're going to love this!"

"Okay..."

"Alright, ready?" Her eyes widen and she pauses again.

"Yes, dammit, would you spit it out!"

"Okay, okay." She takes another sip. "You know my aunt Melanie, right?"

"Uh-huh."

"Well, she owns a condo on the beach, not far from here..." She pauses for a second and when I don't respond, she adds. "I mean she owns the whole building."

"Okay... that's nice for her, I guess." I shrug questioningly.

"Yes it is, and it's nice for us too." She looks at me smiling. "Because she has offered us a unit with ocean view at close to nothing rent!"

I look at her in silence for a second, and then we both scream and kick our feet, attracting strange looks from those sitting around us.

"No way! That's great news!"

"This place is like - right smack on the beach! It's beautiful, it's only six floors high, and the units are pretty big."

"What floor is it on?"

"I think she said unit 508, so it's on the fifth. Can you believe it!" Courtney finishes off her drink.

"How much is the rent?"

"She's asking for only $400, so $200 each." She puts some money on the bill tray the waiter left on our table. "She also said that we would have the option of buying it, we can put the rent money towards the down payment."

"That's great!" Suddenly I find my enthusiasm weaning, as I remember my pathetic jobless situation.

"What's wrong?" She asks frowning.

"Nothing… I just hope I find a job soon, or I might find myself moving back to my parents house in Connecticut, instead of on the beach with you."

"Oh, c'mon, you'll find something, you've sent out a gazillion resumes, someone is bound to call, sweetie."

"Yeah well, when they do call, I never make it passed the 1st interview…"

"That's because they're idiots. Look, let's go take a drive to the beach, and I'll show you the condo." She says eagerly. "I don't have the keys yet, but we can look at it from the outside. It'll definitely cheer you up, and it will inspire you to get hired on your next interview." Not convinced, I agree.

She wasn't kidding; the place is beautiful! It's painted in a dark beige color, with Spanish roof tiles, the front entrance has a waterfall next to it. There's a guard, and then a huge reception area that we can see from the outside. There are palm trees all around, side stairs that lead to the apartments' back doors and a walkway that leads to the beach.

"This is amazing!" I say admiringly.

"Told ya!" She sings. "So how long do you have left on your lease at your current apartment?"

"The lease expires at the end of the month, so I have a couple of weeks."

"Great. I'll try to get out of my current lease early and start moving in and getting it ready for us before you come."

I drive home with renewed optimism. I am determined to get a job, no matter what it takes; I will live in this condo with Courtney, even if I have to sweep floors to pay for it; just not at Readingwrold, of course. I'm so ready to move to the east, my place, although not too bad, is too far west from the ocean and I love the beach too much to be so far away.

As I walk into my apartment, the first thing I do is look at the answering machine. There's one message. I put my purse down, and make a b-line for it.

"Hey sweets, it's me. Call me when you get home." Wow, I'm surprised Ivan's home so early. I quickly dial his number, hoping he hasn't eaten yet.

"Hello?" He answers groggily.

"It's me, I just got home. Were you sleeping?"

"No, no, just watching TV… but I'm starving though."

"Do you want to go eat something?"

These days, Ivan is so busy that we hardly see each other. Going to dinner with him is a huge treat. We go to many functions that his company throws; but too many evenings of stuffy glamour, Filet Mignon and endless superficial chatter with a bunch of lawyers gets old sometimes. I miss a regular night out with just him and I, for dinner, a movie… you know, like a date; but I guess the poor guy is busy, and I understand that.

He picks me up at nine, and we go to Miko's, a diner near my apartment. I tell him all about the condo on the beach, and how desperate I am to get a job. He reassures me that I'll find something, and that he has tons of faith in me. He then tells me about his day, and the hard case he's working on. He's been at a very prestigious law firm for a year now, where he got a job right out of Harvard. Being new in town, a friend of a friend that works with Ivan invited him to a 4th of July party. I met him there and we became friends, and a few weeks later we were dating.

Before Ivan I was like a magnet for top of the line jerks, I seemed to attract the worst losers, so I actually gave up on men for a while. Ivan happened to show up just when I wasn't looking, which in my opinion is the best time to meet the right guy.

"So you guys will be living on the beach, huh?" he says as he spoons the last of his ice cream dessert. "That's really great."

"I can't wait! We'll be on the beach every weekend!"

"Oh, wow, look at the time!" He exclaims as he looks at his watch. "I've got work tomorrow."

A few minutes later Ivan drops me off at my place. I reach over to kiss him goodnight and then ask him if he's staying over.

"I can't, sweets, I've got to go in early tomorrow, and I don't have any work clothes here," he says sounding regretful. I keep forgetting I'm the only loser without a job.

I sigh. "I know, I know… call me tomorrow, and don't work too hard." I pause and then add: "It was good to see you."

"You too," he smiles, "And good luck with the job hunting."

I step out of the car, wave to him and walk into my apartment.

It isn't until I sit on the couch, and turn on the TV, that out of the corner of my eye I notice the answering machine blinking. Hoping it isn't Court saying that the beach condo fell through or something, I press the PLAY button.

"I am calling for Sara Livingston, this is Mrs. Stark from the Human Resources Department of Tivoli-Barnes Advertising Agency," A firm voice says, "We would like to set an appointment for an interview with you sometime this week, preferably tomorrow or the next day. Please call me at 800-555-6578 tonight, if possible, or tomorrow no later than nine – in the morning that is. Thank you."

I play the message back like 4 times; I can't believe it! Tivoli-Barnes is the biggest Ad Agency in the Fort Lauderdale area, they occupy an entire super modern high rise building in downtown. At what time did they call? It's almost passed eleven, I check the message yet again to see the time the call was placed: nine thirty seven. Mmmm, that's kind of late to be calling from an office, isn't it? Oh well, whatever, the fact is that they called!

Two

The alarm clock makes me jolt from a deep and peaceful sleep. I reach over and slam it off, noticing that it is eight thirty a.m. I'm still groggy from having gone to bed at three in the morning because I was re-arranging my portfolio to perfection. I'm still on the 'unemployed schedule', so since I only have to call in to schedule the interview, I can return to bed for a couple more hours after I make the call.

I get up and walk to the living room as I mumble to myself so I can get my voice to sound as if I've been awake for a while. "Yes, this is Sara Livingston, I'm returning your call from – uh…" Okay, do I say last night, evening, yesterday? I decide on 'yesterday' and go on practicing a couple more times.

Okay here goes; I dial the number, after two rings a female voice answers. "Tivoli-Barnes HR Department, this is Ms. Snark speaking."

"Yes, hello, I am Sara Livingston I-"

"I'm sorry, say again?"

"This is Sara Livingston, I'm returning your call from yesterday, you had left a message?"

"In regards to…?"

"About a resume I sent in, you wanted to set an appointment." Could she have forgotten already?

"Are you sure it wasn't Ms. Stark who left the message?"

Huh? Isn't that what I said? "Well… maybe, it's possible, of course." I hope I got the message right.

"Right, yes it was, I'm Ms. Snark, Ms. Stark is the one who usually calls our future prospects." I hear some papers being shuffled. "Hold on one minute, please."

Half a minute goes by, then someone gets on the line again.

"May I help you?"

"Yes, this is Sara Livingston, I'm calling back in regards to the message you left yesterday, to set up an interview."

"Right…, let me see here… one second." There's silence as I hear more shuffling. "Sara… Living-, oh, yes here it is. I'm sorry, we just have a ton of resumes here." She laughs lightly. I throw in a small fake laugh back, and wait for her to continue.

"Okay, so when can you come in?"

"Well, anytime that's good for you, I'm available."

"That's great! They really need someone right away, how about coming in this morning?"

"Uh…" I look at my pajamas, and run a hand through my messy hair. "Sure, no problem."

"Are you far away from us? We're located in downtown Fort Lauderdale."

"No, not too far, how about I come in an hour?"

She hesitates a bit, and then she agrees. "When you come into the lobby, ask for me, and they will give you a Visitor pass. HR's on the 5th floor, third office on the left. Just ask the man at the front desk if you need directions. Okay? See you in about 55 minutes!"

"Okay, see you then, thank you." I answer and she hangs up. Wow, she must really want me to come in. That's a good sign.

I get dressed in record time; good thing I have an outfit set aside for interviews. It is always ready when duty calls, I don't wear it much, so it looks new. I grab my portfolio and I'm out the door. I manage to make it downtown in less than thirty minutes, thanks to light traffic, and a few disregarded amber-to-red lights. Luckily, the Tivoli-Barnes Building has its own covered parking, and I find a spot in the Visitor area pretty quickly.

"Good morning." I say as I enter the lobby and approach the man behind the desk. His name tag says 'Joe', so I address him by that, give him my name and tell him who I am here to see. He looks over a list of names in front of him on his desk.

"I don't see your name here… Is it Ms. Stark, or Ms. Snark you're here to see?" Oh no, here we go again.

"Uh, it's the lady in the HR department, the one that calls the applicants…" I say hoping he knows what I'm talking about.

"Let me call HR, and just give them your name." Good idea, Joe. More than five minutes have gone by now, and this Ms. Snark, or Stark, will think I'm late.

"Okay, I think we got it now, it's Ms. Stark you want to see, she just forgot to put your name on the visitors list for this morning. They are quite busy up there."

"She's on the fifth floor, right?"

"Yes she is, but hold on a minute, I have to give you this visitor sticker." He slowly and carefully writes down my name, and date of visit on a blue sticker, and takes off the backing as he hands it to me. "Just place it somewhere so it's visible."

I take it and stick it on the top right side of my suit jacket. "Thanks."

"Good luck, now. Elevators are straight and to the right."

I make my way up, and after a few walks up and down the hallways of the fifth floor, I finally ask someone to point me to the Human Resources Department. I feel a bit stupid realizing I walked by it at least twice. I stop rehearsing the interview in my head, so that I can pay attention to where I'm going. I walk in and tell the woman behind the desk who I am and she instructs me to sit down on the ultra modern couch that's against the wall. There's a closed door behind her, so I assume that's where the interview will take place.

I'm starting to get a little impatient after 15 minutes of sitting, and can only get a half smile out of the lady behind the desk. It isn't less than 20 minutes later, when she finally says something. "Sorry it's taking a bit long, I'm sure they'll be done any second now." I nod back.

Finally the door opens and a tall, middle aged woman with curly blonde hair emerges. I look up and smile conservatively, waiting for the lucky prospect that probably got the job to come waltzing out of the interview room.

"Please come in." She says holding the door open. I walk in and I'm puzzled when no one comes out. The only other person in the room is another middle aged woman with big glasses and a loose dark brown bun who is sitting behind a huge desk.

"Hello, Sara." The lady with the blonde hair says as she closes the door behind her. "I'm Ms. Stark, and this here is Ms. Snark, we both run the HR Department of Tivoli-Barnes. I'll be interviewing you today, so if you would, please have a seat."

She motions to the chair in front of another big desk on the other side of the room and takes a seat behind it.

"Alright, so you are applying for the Junior Graphic Designer position." She says as she shuffles through some papers in a folder. She takes one out and I notice that it is my resume.

"Yes, I am." I respond, and wait for her to go on.

She asks me a bunch of questions about my schooling and past jobs. I tell her about my Liberal Arts Degree with a major in Graphic Design (I over-emphasize on that one) and all the projects I had done while in school. My job history is not the best, since I really haven't had a job as a designer yet, so I make a point to talk a lot about my degree. I slightly embellish my job at the computer lab while in school, and make it sound much more interesting. I need not mention that the Bookworld job has been completely omitted from my curriculum, which was easy to do, since it only lasted a mere four months anyway.

As I answer her questions she writes remarks on the margin of the resume, and then she also writes in answers on a sheet that, from where I'm sitting, looks like a questionnaire. After almost an hour and what seems like a hundred questions, she finally moves on to tell me about the job.

"The job title, as you know, is Junior Graphic Designer." She reads this off a paper. "Duties, include being there for the team, offering support to the Graphic Designers, as well as the Art and Creative Directors. The Art Department is an extremely important asset to Tivoli-Barnes, and they are incredibly busy. So the Junior Graphic Designer is needed for helping with projects, and lending overall assistance, while learning on the job."

"That sounds great." I smile widely.

"Are there any questions you have about the job, Sara?"

"Actually, um, I was wondering if there is any opportunity for advancement."

"Oh, definitely." She assures me. "There are many avenues for growth with our company, it's all up to you, as to where you want to go."

Wow, this really sounds great. I wonder how many more people they still have to interview.

"Okay, Sara, if you don't have anymore questions, then I think we're done." She says standing up. "We have some more applicants to interview, and then we will call three of you back for a second interview. We'll be in touch in a few days' time."

I practically float on my way back down to the parking lot, flashing a huge smile at Joe as I glide by his desk. I don't realize until I get to the car, that I did not show her my portfolio.

As soon as I get home I dial Ivan's number, but he doesn't answer. So instead I call Courtney.

"That sounds really good, how do you think you did? I mean did they seem interested?"

"It's hard to tell." I sigh. "She sure wrote down a lot of stuff, though."

"That's a good sign."

"So how is the apartment thing going?"

"Great, except those idiots in my current place won't let me out of the lease early. I mean, what's a few weeks?"

"Well, that's okay, we'll just move in at the same time, by then I'll have a job, and we can set the place up together. This way it'll give me time to get everything in order."

"Yeah, I guess you're right. I was just hoping to be living there sooner." She whines. "Hey what are you doing later?"

"I don't know, I called Ivan, but he's not home."

"Why don't you come over, I'm having a girls' thing."

Courtney's famous 'girl things' consist of a night with 4 or 5 women drinking and sharing way too much. But I have to admit, they are always fun.

Three

When I get to Courtney's place, Lydia and Rosie are already there. They're all drinking a bright green concoction of some sort.

"Here, try it." Courtney hands me a green drink of my own. "It's a Kiwi-Lime-Mint Martini."

Rosie moves a pillow out of the way and motions for me to sit next to her on the couch. "So tell me, how did your interview go today?"

I tell her about the whole ordeal and she laughs heartedly. "I remember those days... I'm so glad I work for myself. Listen, whenever you're ready to work freelance I can help."

"I'll keep that in mind." I answer sipping my drink. Although it sounds fantastic, I don't think I'm ready to go on my own. I want to at least get some experience working for a big firm and learn about the business. I think if I get a job at a place like Tivoli-Barnes, I can do just that. A few years and a few promotions later, maybe then I can do some freelance work from home.

"Hey, how's Ivan? I haven't seen him in ages." Lydia joins us on the couch with a blue drink this time.

"He's fine, you know, working as usual." I make a mental note to call him before it gets too late.

I find a moment to slip outside, while the girls are gossiping about some guy Rosie met. I try to dial Ivan's number, but my eyes are swimming on the number pad, thanks to the three different colored Martinis I have swallowed. They taste so good that the alcohol is hardly noticeable, that is, until you try to do something that requires your eyes to focus. After a few tries of dialing different numbers, I stupidly realize that I have him on speed dial. I press the number 'one' key and it starts ringing.

"Hey." He answers after 4 rings.

"Hi, I hope it's not too late to call, I tried you earlier but I got no answer."

"No, that's okay, I worked late, and got home not too long ago. How was your interview?" He asks amid some background noise that sounds like the television.

"It went good, I think. The place is incredible, though. I'll tell you more about it when I see you."

"Where are you?" He asks, probably because of the loud laughs that can be heard in the background.

"I'm at Court's, we're having a 'girls' thing'."

"Right… well, you girls have fun!" He says laughing, he knows how ridiculous we get at our nights at Courtney's. "Hey, uh, mark your calendar for a week from Saturday."

"What's a week from Saturday?" I ask, fearing another night out with the 'lawyers'.

"The Brunson Awards Dinner, it's quite a big deal. I'd love it if you could be there…".

"Sure, Ivan, I wouldn't miss it!" I hope I'm not too transparent with my lack of enthusiasm.

"Thanks, sweets. Hey, you'll have an excuse to go dress shopping, you know how I need to impress the boss!"

I go back inside just as Rosie is telling the girls about her latest date, the one she met through datesonline.com.

"And then he tells me that he can't eat after seven p.m. because he develops terrible gas, he can't eat nuts or chocolate because he gets constipated – so much for the ice cream date I had planned – and he can't eat most fruit because he breaks down in hives…" Rosie's shaking her head and Lydia lets out a big snort of laughter. "And all this I learned on our first meeting! You know where we ended up going?"

Courtney motions for me to sit next to her on the floor, then turns back to Rosie. "Where?"

"The library. We went to the library to get some books on eating better! What the hell kind of date is that?"

"Don't those online dating things ask you all kinds of questions so that you get matched with the right person?" I ask her.

"Well, sure, assuming that you don't make half the stuff up so you sound more interesting!" Lydia says amid sips of a bright red drink.

"I didn't lie, though, honest! I don't know why they keep matching me with all these losers! The worst part is that he was acting as if going to the library on a date to get information for improving digestion was perfectly normal."

Rosie has been trying online dating for about a month now. Ever since I first met her in college, she's been dating disaster after disaster. All she wants is a normal guy that she can have a long relationship with, but she has no luck whatsoever. She insists it's because she's too fat, but I don't think having 10 or 15 pounds extra can really be called overweight. She's just looking in the wrong places and this online thing doesn't sound promising at all.

"Rosie, honey, you have to come man hunting with me." Lydia shakes her head. "I'll get you a real man!"

"I think Rosie wants a real man that will still be a reality after one night!" I tell her, as Rosie nods in agreement.

Lydia sighs and takes a sip of her drink. "Well, I still think you should nix this online dating deal, it's really not the the best idea…"

"You should try it!" I tell her laughing.

"Ahhh, no thanks, casual dates are easy enough to find on my own… I don't want to hear some guy's digestive problems all night long, talk about a turnoff!"

"So you're ditching the whole boyfriend concept for good, eh?" I ask Lydia, referring to her last breakup a few months ago. She swore never to get close to a guy again, after her boyfriend of three years broke off their engagement, only a day after he proposed. She was devastated, but I thought she wasn't serious when she said she never wanted a relationship again.

"For now, and probably for the next ten years. I'm done!" She raises her blue martini in the air. "No more guy inflicted pain!"

Even though we're all against heartbreak, we are not all done with men, yet anyway, but we still raise and clink our colorful glasses to Lydia's toast.

For the past week I've been drinking a few more drinks than usual, and eating way too much. At the same time the fact that I have been completely ignoring the gym, has propelled me to spend one whole hour sweating on the treadmill today. I'm feeling great and refreshed, and when I get to my apartment I'm practically singing as I open my mailbox. I stop in mid-verse when I see it; an envelope from Tivoli-Barnes.

I run up inside, sit on the couch and get ready to open it, but I'm filled with doubt when I realize that when they send a letter, instead of a phone call, its usually to say thanks for applying, but sorry they've found someone better. Trust me, I've received plenty of those. I brace for the worst and open the damn thing. I can't believe it when I read that I, along with 2 others have been selected to return for a second interview!

"Wow, that was really fast." Courtney says as I show her the letter the next day. "Your first interview was only two days ago!"

"I know! Can you believe that?"

"No... but really, how did they get the letter so fast?" She sounds doubtful all of a sudden.

"Well, maybe they decided right after I left, and sent the letter the next morning." I say convinced.

"They must have." Courtney shrugs.

We're eating lunch at the Food Court in the Galleria, which is where Courtney manages a Gap store. She studied Fashion Design, and is currently trying to work her way up to Senior Buyer for the South Florida Gap region. Considering she started as a part-time sales girl, she's not doing bad at all.

"So did you call them to set up the interview?"

"Well, apparently it's already set up for tomorrow, they wrote it in the letter." I say, handing her the letter.

"Damn. These people are really efficient!" She says as she looks at it, and then hands it back. "But what if you were out of town or something, and you got the letter too late?"

"Good question... what if?" I shrug. "Hey, at least I got it, right?"

"And you're going tomorrow!"

"Right!"

"And you'll get the job!"

"Yes!"

I read the letter again and notice that the interview is set for eight in the morning.

"What's wrong?" Courtney asks as she stares at me frowning.

"If I get this job, it means that I will officially be in the workforce. No more making up my schedule, and working afternoon part-time jobs… Hello 9-5 world." I'm suddenly feeling apprehensive.

"Welcome to the real world, sweetie!" Courtney smiles mischievously. "You had to join sooner or later! Hey, you'll probably even have to work over-time, ha-ha!"

"Ugh! Shut up!"

Once again I find myself at the lobby of Tivoli-Barnes. It's almost eight in the morning and I'm half asleep. I spent the night at Ivan's so that it would be easier getting up, since he's out of bed by six; but not even three cups of coffee have helped in waking me up this morning.

"Here you go, Sara." Joe hands me the 'Visitor' sticker. "You're all set."

"Thanks!" I say as I make my way to the elevators.

This time I only have to wait about ten minutes before Ms. Stark, or Ms. Snark – will I ever get them straight? – opens the door. She leads me back into the office, this time I'm instructed to sit on the desk by the entrance.

"Ms. Snark will conduct today's interview, she'll be with you in just a minute. Did you bring your portfolio?"

"Yes, I did." I smile and motion to the little flat briefcase I placed on the floor by the chair. I make a mental note not to forget to show it to them if they don't ask. Ms. Stark walks out of the room, and a second later Ms. Snark walks in. I think I finally know which is which.

"Good morning, Sara, how are you?" She takes a seat behind her desk. We start by going over the history of the company, how long it's been around, who the founders are, etc.

"Mr. Tivoli comes around quite a bit, he still has an office on the top floor, although he has given almost full reign to his son over everything. Mr. Barnes died a few years ago, but his name remains at the request of Mr. Tivoli since he and Mr. Barnes were good childhood friends." Ms. Snark explains as she flips through a file folder.

We talk about the salary, and a bunch of other details that I will soon forget. She then hands me a couple of brochures detailing the company, and explaining the benefits package. She looks at my portfolio rather quickly, and then tells me that when they determine which one of us three candidates will be returning for the third interview, she will be contacting me.

By the time we're done it's ten o'clock. Ivan suggested we have lunch at around twelve being that his office is not too far from the Tivoli-Barnes building. Since I need something to do until noon, I decide to go to the Museum of Art, which is only a five minute walk. I spend a couple of hours admiring a new exhibition by a local artist and then start to make my way to the building where Ivan works.

I never really liked going to Ivan's offices, because the whole environment is so stiff over there. Generally speaking, I don't like lawyers, I find most of them to be quite arrogant, which is the reason I didn't believe Ivan at first when he told me what his profession was.

"Good afternoon, can I help you?" Even though I've been here numerous times, the receptionist refuses to remember who I am.

"Hi, Eve. I'm here to see Ivan."

"Ivan McKenzie?"

"Yes." I roll my yes, I mean there's only one Ivan in the whole office.

She dials his office and announces someone is here to see him. A couple of minutes go by and he finally comes out and I notice he's frowning.

"Sara! Gosh I'm so sorry..." he walks me to the other end of the reception area. "I can't make it. We just got called into court. I know I should've called you, I'm really sorry, but this case is really huge, and the judge changed the time at the last minute... We're leaving here in like five minutes."

"I wish you would have said something, Ivan..."

"I know, I know. I am so sorry. I promise I'll make it up to you." With that he gives me a quick kiss on my forehead, and starts to walk back to his office. "I'll call you tonight, sweets, ok?"

I turn to leave, but not before I see Eve smirk as she quickly turns her attention to a stack of papers in front of her. I shake my head and walk toward the elevator.

Four

I've been to four stores and still haven't seen any dress that's halfway decent. I could kick myself for having waited until literally the last minute to go shopping for a ball gown. The awards dinner for Ivan's law firm is in less than 2 hours, and I'm really getting desperate to find something.

I decide to stop at the Gap, despite my better judgment to continue my dress search; but I need a break. When I walk into the store I find Courtney showing a new sales girl how to fold a sweater.

"Hey!" She looks at me in surprise. "Shouldn't you be home getting ready?

I'm about to tell her my dilemma, when a stream of giggles comes out of Courtney's sweater folding pupil. We both look at her as she holds up a lump of wool with a sleeve coming out of it's middle. "This just doesn't look right!" More giggles. "What did I do wrong?"

Courtney rolls her eyes sideways at me, so the girl doesn't see her, and then folds the sweater one more time very slowly talking her through every fold.

"Do you think you can try again, Dee Dee?" Courtney asks in the most patient tone I have ever heard her use.

"Um, I think so." She giggles again when she drops the sweater on the floor. She picks it up, and goes at it again.

We leave a very concentrated Dee Dee to her folding, and go to the back of the store where we can talk.

"Having trouble finding good help?" I ask mocking her a little bit.

"She seemed apt when I first interviewed her…" She complains.

"I guess I can see why Tivoli-Barnes likes to interview a hundred people!"

"Still haven't heard from them?" Courtney actually looks concerned. "Hey, there's always sweater folding at the Gap!"

"It seems as if that may be all I'm skilled to do."

It's been over a week now since my last interview with Ms. Stork, and I haven't heard anything. Then again, I haven't gotten a rejection letter either. That could be a good sign – or a bad one, I guess; they may just have hired someone and are so busy that they cannot bother to write letters to the rejects.

"You'll find something, Sara, c'mon don't give up. Besides, you can't be all bummed out tonight, you have to look your best for Ivan's awards thing!"

"Shit, I almost forgot about tonight! I've been to every store that sells dresses. I'll just have to put on something I've already worn, and Ivan will be embarrassed by the fact, even though he won't say anything." I sigh loudly.

"Well that's just too bad for him! Honestly Sara, if that's what he worries about-"

I cut her off not wanting to get a lecture on Ivan's sensitivity, or lack thereof. "Look, I know, but right now I need a dress, and I'm running out of time!"

"Have you tried Inga's?"

"Ing-who? Sounds like old ladies clothes..." I grimace.

"Are you nuts! They have super exclusive clothes!" She then lowers her voice to tell me that she wouldn't be working at the Gap if they'd hired her at Inga's.

"They have gowns?"

"Sweetie, they have an incredible line of gowns! They're not cheap, though, but they are completely unique."

Without hesitation I head over to Inga's. I'm not in the best position to spend a lot of money right now, but I decide that I have no choice. As soon as I walk through the dorr of Inga's a realize Courtney was not kidding, within minutes I find an absolutely gorgeous floor length gown. The sales lady eyes me suspiciously as I go into the fitting room. It's quite a snobby place, but I think Courtney could've done alright here. She would've knocked the attitude out of every stuffy sales woman in the place. Come to think of it, that's probably why they didn't hire her.

I try on the gown and I can't believe it fits and it looks decent. I avoid looking at anything else, for fear I'll find another great looking dress and spend an hour deciding. I take it to the woman at the register and she makes a sour face through the whole process of ringing it up. I almost choke when she tells me the total, but I try to act totally neutral as I hand her my credit card. I should just tell her that my lawyer boyfriend gave me money to buy it. When she hands me the bag with the dress, she barely says thank you. "Whatever." I sigh shaking my head, and grab the bag.

I get home with exactly twenty-seven minutes to get ready. I take a record fast shower, get dressed and apply some make up, and I thank the stars that Ivan isn't here yet. I still have to style my hair, and don't know what to do with it.

I have just started blow drying it, when the doorbell rings. I open the door and there, standing in a very elegant and expensive looking suit is my boyfriend. His blond hair is freshly cut, parted to the side, his tall frame falls perfectly into his dark grey jacket. His blue eyes really stand out, and he smells wonderful. He whistles when he sees my dress, but then he looks at my hair questioningly.

"I haven't done my hair yet, but I'm pretty much ready." I tell him before he can say anything.

"Oh, okay." He sounds frazzled and chuckles nervously. "Because we're supposed to be there at seven thirty."

I assure him I'll be just a minute, and decide to do the only thing feasible at this point. I apply some anti-frizz stuff and comb it in; then I end up using the whole bottle to make sure it will work. My hair is a bit sticky, but it reacts well when I scrunch it with my hands. I pull the front section back and secure it with a silver clasp, then I do a last look in the mirror and I'm done. I grab a silk black jacket and my purse, and we're out the door.

"You look great, sweets." Ivan says as we make our way into the Macon Hotel. It must be true, because he sounds like he means it. I hope my hair won't frizz up as it usually does when I don't blow dry it, but it seems like the anti-frizz serum really took hold. The gala is being held at the Grand Ballroom Suite; and like with all the awards dinners Ivan's firm throws, the place looks fantastic.

We walk into the ballroom and find our table, but not before we stop and say hello to everyone we encounter on the way. We put our jackets down on the chairs and head towards the open bar. On the way there we keep stopping to talk to more people, Ivan seems ecstatic to be here, he's so excited that he keeps forgetting to introduce me to the ones I don't know.

"Let's get that drink!" He says as we find ourselves close enough to the bar before we get stopped again.

"It's rude not to introduce me, you know?" I complain.

"Oh, I didn't introduce you? I'm so sorry, sweets." He says concerned. "What a dope I am, it's just that I'm a little distracted by all this, you know… What do you want? A White Russian?"

"Sweet Martini."

We take our drinks back to our table and almost make it without interruption. Almost. We run into Ivan's boss, the senior partner, and his new wife, whom I've never met. Ivan shakes Mr. Rubious hand and then takes his new wife's and kisses the back of it. I try hard not to think that he's over doing it, but my feelings get the better of me. He regally asks her how she's doing, and I nudge him with my elbow.

"Oh, this here is my girlfriend, uh, Sara." He puts his hand on my shoulder.

I smile uncomfortably. "A pleasure, Mrs. Rubious."

They go on talking for a while, and I find this an excellent time to excuse myself to go to the ladies room. I take my time walking around checking out the place. Even though I can't wait until the evening is over, I still like the feeling of walking around wearing this beautiful gown in such an elegant hotel. I make a few more rounds until I go into the women's lounge.

I am adjusting my hair clasp, when I notice a slight re-growth under my armpits. Shit, just wonderful, that's what I get when I try to hurry up in the shower. Luckily it's not jungle long, but it's enough to be noticed at very close range. I make a mental note to keep my arms down for the rest of the evening. Good thing Ivan and I usually don't dance at these things since he's always busy talking to everyone.

"Sara!" I see Ivan making his way towards me as I enter back into the ballroom. "Where've you been? I was looking for you!"

"Why?" I didn't think he would notice if I was gone for a few minutes.

"Well, Mr. Lowery was looking for someone to dance with, since his wife had just recently fractured her foot." He tells me all excited as he leads me back to our table.

"Sara would love to dance with you, Mr. Lowery." Ivan tells him smiling. "She's a great dancer." Mrs. Lowery, who is sitting next to her husband, obviously uncomfortable with a huge cast on her foot, does not look very happy.

I force a smile and follow Mr. Lowery to the dance floor as I try hard not to show my discomfort. Mr. Lowery has somewhat of a reputation for being a little fresh, if you know what I mean. He's pretty harmless, but his ogling goes more than noticed. Everyone laughs it off, and just calls him overly friendly. Of course, that may be for the little fact that he's seventy percent owner of the firm. Also, as it turns out, he's quite effective in the courtroom when women judges are presiding; apparently they find him 'adorable'.

As Mr. Lowery spins me around in a twirl, I manage to take a quick look over at Ivan. He's sitting next to Mrs. Lowery, who's frowning face is looking straight at me. Just as I'm forced to turn the other way by one more twirl, I catch another glimpse of Ivan; is he trying to 'chair dance' with Mrs. Lowery? Before I can figure out what he's doing, I find myself facing Mr. Lowery again, who's grinning and staring at my chest. I quickly turn sideways, reminding myself to keep my arms down, although somehow I doubt he'll notice my underarms. He's indiscreetly staring at my butt as I do another turn and come to face him again.

I sigh gratefully when dinner is finally announced and we have to go sit down. I go back to the table where most people are in their seats, but Ivan's nowhere to be seen. I grab my jacket and quickly put it on, thankful to have it to conceal my dreaded armpit stubble. When they start serving Ivan still isn't back, I take a look around and finally spot him at the other end of the room talking to someone. He realizes that just about all the tables are starting to eat so he finally makes his way back.

He sits down and kisses me on the cheek. "Hi sweets, how're you doing?"

"Good." I say, and then lowering my voice I add, "The dancing was quite interesting."

He frowns for a second before he answers. "Oh, yeah… how did that go?"

I start to tell him about my underarm problem, but I'm interrupted when Mr. Rubious gets his attention to ask him something.

The dinner goes by without incident, and soon after comes the dessert and coffee. As they usually do in these events, when they begin serving the dessert they also start to set up the podium for the awards ceremony. I'm on my second éclair when the presenter is well into the ceremony. I'm about to take a bite when I hear him say Ivan's name, I put my fork down and begin to clap. I turn to give him a hug but he's already walking up to the podium with a wide smile on his face.

"Mr. McKenzie is part of the South Florida team." The presenter says as Ivan joins him on the stage. "His work in the Revis case has been magnificent, without his hard work the firm would have had to spend quite a bit of additional time on the proceedings. I can say without fault, that I envision Mr. McKenzie as being an essential member to this firm fro years to come!" The whole room breaks into applause and stands up. When they sit back sown, Ivan is left to make his speech.

He does it quite effortlessly, and I can see why he's so great at what he does. He finishes it off with a very nice touch, "Ladies and gentleman, I'd like to thank Mr. Rubious and Mr. Lowery for giving me the opportunity to work at such a prestigious and eloquent law firm. Rubious & Lowery is by far one of the most ethical firms in the country and it is by all means due to the integrity and substance you both hold so dear."

Ivan makes his way back to the table while a huge applause erupts all around. He's all smiles as he shakes hands with his peers, and sits back down.

"Congratulations sweetie!" I tell him as he turns to me.

"Thanks sweets!" He kisses me on the cheek. "I'm so happy you could make it, thanks for being here. And for looking so gorgeous." He adds as he raises one eyebrow while looking me over with a devilish smile.

"You're looking quite the guy yourself, hotshot!" I say, admiring how good he looks in his power suit. There's just something about a man, specially a young and gorgeous one like Ivan, in a suit. He smiles and turns back toward the stage as the room quiets down for the next award.

After about an hour of boring acceptance speeches, the music comes on again, and the dance floor re-opens. A couple of Ivan's colleagues get up to dance and invite us to come along. Ivan hesitates at first, but I convince him to come out and dance at least one song. We stay for a couple of minutes and then Ivan sees someone he wants to talk to, so I excuse myself to go get a drink. I'm almost back at the table when a reddish faced and grinning Mr. Lowery grabs my arm.

"Well, well, young lady," He slurs slightly and then sips from his cocktail. "What do you say to getting this old man's heart pumping a bit again?"

"Um, I'd love to, Mr. Lowery," I think quickly. "But, uh, I think your wife wanted you for something."

His face straightens up, and he looks around the room. "Hadelaide? Oh, where is she?" I point towards their table. Really, how far can the woman get with a broken foot? I quickly walk away before he can say anything else and make my way to the ladies' room. Not wanting to go back into the ballroom, I take a few more walks around the hotel lobby. I sneak back in to get a drink from the bar, and noticing Ivan talking to Mr. Rubious and a few others, I quickly walk back out to the lobby with my drink. Although I feel kind of alone, the time I spend walking by myself around the lobby is the most fun I have all night.

Five

Joey smiles as he hands me the 'Visitor' sticker. "Good luck."

"Thanks." I smile back, slapping the label onto my jacket. This time I am to go straight to the Art Department, which is on the 10th floor. I just hope this interview won't be as long as the others, because I can hardly keep my eyes open.

Ms. Stark called at 7:45 this morning, three weeks after the last interview. She sounded almost out of breath when she said she wanted me to be in by 8:00am for my third and last interview. Since that was an impossibility, I persuaded her to make it 8:30am instead. This is still early, but at least it gave me time to put some clothes on and get the sleepy look off my face. Since Courtney had off today, and I was still in my perpetual state of unemployment, we decided to go out last night. We didn't get home until nearly four in the morning, so when my phone rang just 3 hours after I'd gotten to bed, I was not about to answer it. When the machine picked up and there was Ms. Stark's voice, it took all I had to drag myself out of bed and click on the Talk button.

The first thing I notice when I get off the elevator is the amazing view of the city. The windows are huge and they extend almost from floor to ceiling, making it all bright and airy. I approach the receptionist's desk and tell her why I'm here.

"Please have a seat, Neil will be right out." She says, not looking up from something she's reading.

"Thanks." I smile, to no one in particular since she's still looking down, then I sit on the modern couch next to the reception desk. While I wait, I look through some of the samples of the work done by the Art department, the brochures look pretty amazing.

"Sara?" I look up and see a man standing by the couch. He's wearing a beige hippyish linen shirt and matching pants. He looks to be in his late forties, with a trimmed beard and blondish wavy shoulder length hair.

"Yes!" I say standing up and grabbing my portfolio. "Hello."

"I'm Neil the Art Director, how are you?"

"Nice to meet you, I'm doing great, thanks." We shake hands.

"Please, follow me." He leads me through an archway behind the reception desk and we come into a hallway where the walls are all decorated in framed advertisements and brochures. We go by a room surrounded by glass and inside are a bunch of high tech printers and scanners. We keep going and pass some offices until we come to an open door. He gestures me to go in and follows closing the door behind him. It's a huge room decorated in a mix of modern office furniture and Hindu looking artifacts. In one corner there's a large desk with the latest model Macintosh desktop computer on top, and an ultra sleek Macintosh laptop next to it.

"Please sit down." He motions to a chair by the desk and takes a seat on the other side. "Welcome to your third interview."

"Thank you, its great to be here." I smile with confidence. Courtney told me to appear confident because it shows initiative.

He takes a sheet of paper from a manila folder, which looks to be my resume. He studies it and nods as he goes through it holding his glasses with the other hand.

"I see, mhmmm. Okay… okay…" He nods slowly and bites the earpiece of the glasses and looks the paper up and down. "So you've recently graduated, and earned a Liberal Arts degree in Graphic Art?"

"Yes, sir, just last May."

He then asks to see my portfolio, and goes through it pretty quickly.

"Very good, very good." He hands me back the portfolio. "Well, as you know the job opening is for the Junior Graphic Designer. I believe that you possess the right skills for the job, so let me tell you what would be expected if we were to offer you the position."

I try hard not to smile too widely. "Of course."

"Since we're so busy," he puts a lot of emphasis on the word 'so', "we need someone who can help the designers with all aspects of their projects. Also, as a Junior, you'd be assisting the department in general. As you grow into the position we'd be delegating different tasks to you once you become more familiar with how things are done. In doing so, you'd learn how our projects are completed, and would be training for, eventually, handling a possible project on your own. Does that sound like something you could manage?"

"Definitely, it sounds excellent." I say firmly. It does sound good, even the parts where I'm not too sure what he means, like 'assisting the department in general', but overall it sounds like the perfect job, specially for just starting out.

"Okay then, let me take you on a tour of the department." He starts to get up, and I do the same. "Ms. Stork will be in contact with you as to the final confirmation of the position, the starting date and salary." He continues as he holds the door open.

"Alright, thank you." I say following him out of the office. He takes me around the department, which apparently occupies the whole 10th floor. There are so many rooms, and equipment that I can see it will take a while to learn my way around. At the end of the tour, though, I realize that he hasn't shown me where my work area will be, so I don't know if I get an office or just a desk somewhere. Although, overall the place seems magnificent!

"Congratulations! A toast to you!" Courtney lifts up her martini glass while we sit on the floor by her coffee table, I lift mine and we toast in mid air. "When do you start?"

"Ms. Stork, or Stark, I get them confused, will call me to give me the details on that."

"Great!" she exclaims taking a sip of her cocktail. "What does Ivan say?"

"I haven't told him yet." I say and she looks at me frowning. "I called him at the office earlier, but he was in court, and when I called again later he was in the middle of a meeting and couldn't talk. He also said he'd be working pretty late tonight, so I haven't had a chance." I say reassuringly.

Courtney shakes her head, and smirks. "I swear that boy loves his job way too much. Either that or he has a girlfriend on the side."

"Why the hell would you say that for?" I know she's kidding, but it still bugs me that she said it.

"Relax, he can hardly hang on to one girlfriend, I doubt he'd have two!" She laughs. "Besides, he's not dedicated enough."

"Dedicated?"

"Well, I'm dedicated, so I have two boyfriends sometimes…"

"Yeah, but you don't sleep with both of them, and sometimes not even with one!"

"By dating two, or three even, I can find the right one in less time and I still maintain my dignity." She smirks and takes a gulp of her drink. Not seeing how this relates to Ivan not being dedicated enough and not really wanting to know, I change the subject.

"Right… Anyway, so moving day is still next week, right?" I ask her.

"Yup! Be ready. Lydia's friend has a pick-up, so he'll come to your place to get your stuff first and then to mine. Is three in the afternoon good for you?"

"That's fine." I hadn't given too much thought as to what things I'd be moving. All the furniture in my current apartment belongs to the landlord, all I have are books and clothes. "You know, I think I'll need to do some furniture shopping."

"Actually, I really don't have any furniture either." she says and turns on the laptop computer on the coffee table. "We could order some stuff from IKEA, what do you think?"

"Well, why not? I have a job now… we might as well!"

We spend the next few hours ordering a whole apartment's worth of furnishings, and charging it to both our credit cards. Hey, the investment is worth it if we're going to own this new beach place one day.

It's been two days since my third interview, and I'm finally going to tell Ivan the whole story. I mean I told him on the phone yesterday that I got the job, but that's all I could say before he had to go into a meeting. We made plans to go to dinner tonight and he's picking me up in ten minutes. Ms. Stark called this morning and told me I'd be starting tomorrow. The salary is not spectacular, but for starters it's quite enough to pay the bills, as well as the occasional night out.

"They asked you to start on a Thursday?" Ivan asks as we look through the menu.

"Well, she said that this way I could get two days on the job training, before starting full force on Monday."

"I see." He answers, not looking up from his menu.

We order some appetizers and drinks, and sit in silence for a couple of minutes.

"How's work going for you?" I ask him trying to start some conversation.

"Great, it's going really good actually." He tells me enthusiastically. He then goes on all about his latest case for a client that is suing a stock trading company. About five minutes in I lose track of the story, I keep nodding, but I really don't understand much of the lawyer language, and I don't want to ask for fear that it may instigate an even longer story. Ivan obviously loves his work and it's all he talks about, he gets bored quickly with conversations unless they contain something law related. Many times he's even turned subjects that have nothing to do with law, into potential court cases. He has annoyed most of my friends in such conversations, but they just make light of it and try not to take it too personally.

Some say I'm too patient with him; I just think that Ivan is very talented, and even though sometimes he may get a little overwhelming it's great that he's so passionate about his career.

"Sara, did you hear me?"

"Huh? Oh, I'm sorry I was just thinking about my new job, what was that again?"

"I said that I may not be able to help you move on Saturday, because Mr. Rubious has asked me to look over some affidavits for this case so I can be ready for court on Monday."

"Oh." That I heard. "Well… I guess we'll manage. Lydia's friend is helping us, besides I don't have that much stuff to move anyway."

Our food arrives, and although meat ravioli is my favorite I'm not particularly hungry anymore. I guess I ate too much of the appetizers.

"Mmm, this is good! How's yours?" Ivan asks as he sips his wine.

I force a smile. "Oh, it's wonderful."

Six

I wake up to Ivan's alarm clock and look at the time: 5:30am. Yuck! I drag myself out of the covers and head for the bathroom. Ivan is still asleep, since he doesn't have to be up for at least an hour. I stayed over last night, because Ms. Stark asked me to be in by 7:00am on my first day, and Ivan lives closer to downtown, I also took the opportunity to spend some time with him, since I hardly ever see him as it is.

By the time I'm ready it's half passed six, I kiss Ivan goodbye and head for the door.

"Good luck on your first day, sweets." He mumbles from his bed, still half asleep. "Call me later."

"Good morning," I smile at the receptionist who doesn't seem to remember me from my last interview. "I'm Sara and I'm here for my first day of work..."

She looks down at her appointment book on the desk. "Oh yes, Sara here you are... please wait and I'll get Neil." She calls in to Neil's office, and in a few minutes he comes out. We walk into the hallway and he takes me down the long corridor, but this time we don't go through the glass printer room, but straight on the corridor and go to the very end of it.

"This here is your office." He turns the light on, and motions with his arm for me to go in. "Please settle in first and then meet me back in the conference room in a half hour so you can meet the rest of the team and we can also go over your responsibilities."

"Alright, no problem." I tell him.

I look around the tiny windowless office, and realize that it really isn't an office, but a closet. It doesn't have a door and one of the walls is a partition that separates it from what seems to be a big room on the other side. I look through the cracks of the partition and see a lot of shelves with what looks to be printer supplies and reams of paper. Hey, at least it's partly private, most junior Graphic Designers don't even get a cubicle. I put my purse inside the desk drawer and notice that there are still a few things inside. Lots of paper clips, a bunch of plastic supermarket bags, some highliters among a bunch of café and deli menus. I throw out what I don't need, and keep what could be useful.

Next, I turn on the computer, it makes a loud noise before the monitor lights up. It's a Power Computing model from some years back when Apple allowed a few companies to make Mac clones. I hope the thing still works.

I assume that this is something temporary and when they start assigning me more projects they'll get me something more up to date. I mean, otherwise I won't be able to design as much as a business card on this fossil. I go through all the files in the hard drive to see what kind of programs are in here. Remembering that I have to go to the conference room, I glance at the computer clock and see that I have about a minute left before the half hour is up.

I start making my way down the long corridor, and realize that I don't know where this conference room is. No one is around, and the offices seem empty, I start to panic thinking that they all must be waiting for me in this conference room somewhere. I'm just about to walk down to the lobby to ask Joe if he knows where the damn conference room is, when a tall woman with a reddish bob comes towards me.

"There you are!" she leads me forward. "Neil realized that you probably didn't know where the conference room was! I'm Carol by the way, welcome to the team!"

"Thanks, nice to meet you Carol." I start to ask her what her position is when she opens the door to a big conference room and motions for me to go on in. Six people are sitting down on a long oval table, all looking at me. I smile awkwardly and look for an empty chair.

"Everyone, this is Sara, the new 'Junior'" Neil announces as I sit down. He goes on to tell me everyone's names and their titles, which I try hard to memorize. I'm terrible with names, I hope I'll learn who's who before too long. Did he say 'Junior'?

The guy next to me, I think is Larry, Senior Graphic Designer, must have noticed my confusion and leans over. "Junior is for Junior Graphic Artist." Oh. Duh. I nod in acknowledgement.

"Now, let's just go over the progress of our standing projects, this way Sara can get an idea of how we operate." Neil opens a manila folder and takes out some sheets of paper. "Okay, let's see here… the Albright account, Amy how's that coming along?" I think Amy is a Senior Art Director. If I heard correctly, there are like two Senior Art Directors, as well as two Art Directors. There's only one Creative Director, Neil, then there's also an Imaging Specialist, which I think is Carol, the receptionist and the "Junior" – me.

"I have the preliminary computer sketches completed, but I need the text typed up. I also need to scan in the logo and color correct it." She quickly answers.

"Sounds good," Neil says, slowly scratching his chin. "Mmmm, how about… how about you let Sara type up the text, and scan the logo, would that help?" He takes his glasses off and casually chews on the earpiece as he looks at Amy.

"Sure, that'd be great." She nods firmly.

"Sara?" Neil looks over at me, still chewing on his earpiece. "Would that be something you could handle?"

"Yes, of course, I can do that."

As the meeting goes on I get assigned a few more tasks. I can't help but feel that the jobs that are being delegated to me are the less desirable ones that they rather not do. But, hey, that's what I'm here for; I'm the 'Junior', I have to start somewhere. As I go on to prove myself on the job, they'll have me doing more interesting stuff. After all, that's what Ms. Stark – or Ms. Stork – insinuated in the interview.

"I think that's it for this morning, guys," Neil says standing up. "And don't forget, lunch today in honor of our new colleague."

I realize that we've been in this meeting for over two hours, I wonder if they have them every morning; or maybe it's just because it is my first day here and all. My train of thought is interrupted when Amy taps me on the shoulder as I walk back to my new office.

"When you're ready, please come to my office, and I'll show you what you need to do, okay?" She smiles curtly.

"Oh, sure, I can come now." I suggest.

"Do you have your pen and paper?"

I tell her that I don't have any supplies, and I'm not sure where to get them. She looks a little annoyed and sighs heavily.

"Come with me." She says as she abruptly turns on her heel and walks down the hallway. "Neil? Neil! Sara hasn't been given any supplies or anything! I thought that was taken care of?" She demands.

Neil calmly comes out of his office. "Mmmmm... well let me see if Marcia can get them for her." He tells me to go with him as he goes to the front reception area.

"Just come to my office when you get the stuff then." Amy says after another heavy sigh. "Oh, my office is two doors down from Neil's." She says pointing to the direction of what I assume is her office.

The receptionist, Marcia, gets a bunch of supplies out of a locked closet and puts them in a large bag. She looks to be in her early twenties, she's slightly plump with a too low neckline, a short skirt, dark frizzy curly hair and very red lipstick.

"Here you go." She hands me the bag and turns to sit back down by the reception desk.

"Thanks, Marcia."

"Yeah." She responds as the phone rings and looks at it before picking it up on the 3rd ring.

"Okay, that's better!" Amy tells me as I walk in her office with my brand new notepad and pen. She then, goes over all the steps to access the database, shows me where all the files are and gives me the logos to scan. She also gives me the text I have to input for her project. All 10 pages of it. When she's done with me, it's almost time for lunch. We eat in the Art Department's mini-cafeteria, Art is the only department in the company to have its own cafeteria, that being because it's the only department to have the whole floor, besides the executive offices upstairs.

They ordered lunch from an Italian restaurant and it's incredibly good, it tastes pretty expensive. We even have tiramisu for dessert. I wonder if they do this every time someone new is hired, nonetheless, it makes me feel pretty good.

I spend the rest of the afternoon with Tim, who is the company's Systems Administrator. Apparently my computer isn't accessing the database, it turns out it was disconnected from the network. After Tim connects it he realizes he has to erase everything and reconfigure the computer, so he has to install all the programs again. He works in silence as if I'm not there, and just nods or shakes his head when I ask him questions. I get the feeling I'm keeping him from more important work, but I can't do anything unless I can connect to the database, and he's the only one that can fix it. So I hope I don't get too much on his bad side so early on my employment. When he's finally done, Amy comes into the 'closet' asking if I have typed the text and scanned the logos. I explain the computer problems I've been having, but she still seems a bit concerned that I haven't even started yet.

"Well, try and type as much as you can before you leave today, please." She turns and starts to leave, but re-tracks and leans over the doorway. "Just for future reference, if the network is down the computer with the scanner in the printer room has a CD burner, so you can save your scans on a disk and you don't have to depend on sending them through the network."

"Oh, okay, thanks Amy. I'll have the scans done." I try to sound positive. "When do you need them by?"

"Well, today would've been nice, but tomorrow morning's fine." She smiles curtly and walks away.

It's 5'30 in the afternoon, and just as I'm wondering if it's getting close to quitting time Neil comes in through the doorway.

"So... how's it going?" He takes off his glasses. "Is everything fine? You like it so far?"

"Great, everything's great." I smile. "Tim helped me set up the computer and the network."

"Good, good..." He starts to chew the glasses. "Mmmmm, I don't know if I had mentioned it... but one of the Junior's responsibilities is to shut off all the printers, the scanners and the wax machines at the end of the day. Did I... mention that at all?"

"No, no I don't think you did," I say and quickly add, "but of course that's no problem."

He takes me to the printer room and shows me how to shut everything off. There's an order that has to be followed, which is kind of confusing, but I write everything down on my notebook, where I already have three pages filled with Amy's notes from earlier.

"Now... our normal hours are from eight to five thirty, but of course... since we're so busy we usually end up staying a bit later. So... you'd be expected to wait until the last person leaves before shutting off the printers and everything."

"Oh, alright, sure." I wish Ms. Stork – or Stark – would've mentioned this... Oh well, it can't be too bad.

"Also… you're expected to come in at seven thirty, before everyone arrives, and turn everything on." He puts his glasses back on. "It takes the wax machine a good half hour to warm up, should anyone need to use it."

"Ah-ha, okay." It's just temporary, before I know it I'll be promoted.

"I'll give you a key to the printer room, we lock it up every night." He pauses for a few seconds and continues, "Mmmmmm, I was going to have Larry shut the machines off today, but he had to leave early, so I thought it would be good for you to go ahead and get some practice."

He then tells me that David, who I believe is one of the Senior Graphic Designers, is staying late to finish up an important project.

"So… you think you can stay until he's done, and shut things off, would that be alright?"

"Sure, of course." I manage a weak smile. Well, I guess now I can scan that logo, and get started on the text for Amy after all.

Seven

"Okay, the last box!" I breathe a sigh of relief as I drop a box of clothes on the floor of my new room. "I just love it!" I say, looking around the room for the tenth time.

"I know," Courtney walks over to my window and looks out. "It pays to be my friend, doesn't it?"

I walk over to the window as well. I have a partial view of the ocean from my room, and it looks fantastic against the twilight sky. "We can be on the beach in one minute, no more driving and finding parking for an hour!"

"And we can go walking in the afternoons after work, I hear it's great exercise to walk on sand."

"I just hope I don't have to stay at work passed eight every evening…" I say thinking of that little detail not mentioned in the interview.

"You did leave by seven thirty last night, didn't you?" She says trying to be positive. "I mean, you probably won't have to stay that late every single night; besides, the beach is right here! Even if you come late all we have to do is walk downstairs."

"Or I can look at the ocean from my room, or smell it from the balcony…" Hey, I guess we can't have everything, and at least I have a job with which to pay to live here.

At about 8:30 Ivan calls to let me know that just as he thought, he won't be able to make dinner. He called earlier feeling bad that he wasn't able to help with the moving and said he'd try to be here by eight if he could get done with work early enough.

Even though I know Ivan really loves his work, I can't help but feel a little bothered that we have such limited time together. I'd hate to think that if we are to stay together for a long time it would always be like this. Then again, I guess he's just trying to impress his bosses because he's still a newbie.

I sigh heavily and try to think of something else. As I put the last of my books away, a knock on my door makes me look up as Courtney walks in.

"Hey, I thought you would have left for dinner by now," She walks in and sits on my new bed. I tell her about Ivan not coming and she makes a face. "Oh well. Listen I haven't eaten yet either, what do you say we grab some sandwiches, a bottle of wine and have dinner by the waves?"

This actually sounds pretty good. After I find my blanket size towel we put all the food in a cooler and make our way downstairs to the beach. There are still some beachgoers left from the day who are slowly packing their things. To the left of us there are some volleyball players wrapping up their game as they drink beer from a cooler. The light breeze and the smell of the ocean feel very soothing as we eat our turkey sandwiches. If there's one thing for certain, I'm really happy to be able to live here. As we drink some wine and bask in the greatness of it all, the volleyball players walk passed us as they leave. This leaves Courtney and I pretty much the only ones left on the beach.

"I didn't realize it was so late!" I say looking at my watch.

Courtney stares ahead silently and then turns towards me. "Sara, I don't want to butt in, but are you sure that Ivan… I mean he's hardly ever around."

My good mood is now squashed by Courtney's comment. Although, honestly, I can't blame her for being worried because, surely, the guy is a definite workaholic.

"I know he's not, but I understand the pressure of his work." I try to explain. "It's how his job is."

Courtney looks at me for a second before she answers. "Look, I'm sorry, I shouldn't-"

"Hey, it's fine, I'd be mad too if I didn't know better. But I'm sure once he gains confidence from his boss, he'll be able to back down a little and have more time for himself. I mean if he doesn't, we will be having a talk!" I feel reassured after I say this, or at least mostly; I am actually feeling a little neglected. The rest of the evening goes by pretty uneventfully, we watch a movie and then I go to bed feeling pretty exhausted.

"Idiots! Dummies!" Courtney's voice resonates through the apartment as it unpleasantly wakes me up. "Ugh! This sucks!"

I lazily get out of bed and stroll into the living room to make sure everything is all right. Although, if my knowledge of Courtney's ease at reaching fits doesn't fail me, it probably isn't anything to worry about.

"The damn phone people didn't connect the line!" she whines when she sees me walk into the room. "And my cell phone's dead, I can't find the charger, I can't make any calls..."

"How long have you been up?" I ask as I hand her my cell phone.

"I don't know, couldn't sleep..." She starts dialing. "What time is it anyway?"

"Almost ten." I yawn. Way too early to be getting up on a Sunday. I walk into the kitchen and start a pot of coffee.

"Hey Sara," Courtney calls from the living room. "Do you know you have messages on your cell phone?"

I finish making the coffee and bring two cups into the living room. The first message is from Ivan, he must have called when we were at the beach last night. He can't make the movies tonight. I'm surprised when I listen to the second message and hear Neil's voice. Apparently he wanted to know if I could come in today, but not to worry if I already had plans. He knew it was short notice and understood if I couldn't make it. He goes on for about five minutes explaining that even though I'm not really involved in the project they need to work on, it was indirectly tied to the text I wrote for Amy on my first day. Evidently, I didn't write all of it, there were a couple of paragraphs at the end that I missed.

Because of the missing text the whole design of the brochure has to be redone, and the client is expecting to see it tomorrow first thing. He assures me again that it's okay if I can't come in, but he asks if I can call anyway when I get the message. It strikes me as strange that he didn't ask me to come in yesterday.

"On a Sunday? That's kind of strange." Courtney asks. "Are you gonna call him back?"

"Well... I don't know. I mean I don't have any reason why I couldn't go in, so if I call I'll have to go."

"Just tell him you had plans, make something up."

"Yeah, but you know me... I'm a terrible liar."

"Well just tell him tomorrow you had your phone turned off all weekend, and you never got the message." Courtney says ingeniously as she finishes her coffee.

"That's lying isn't it?"

"Argh Sara! You have to loosen up!" Courtney whines. "By the way, since you're not going to the movies with Ivan, you're coming with us tonight, right?"

"I could use a night out I guess, sure."

I end up going in to work. I just feel that I'm too new to dodge work unless it's legitimate. Fortunately, it is not as bad as I anticipated and Amy doesn't blame me for not having the text, or so Neil tells me. Amy wasn't able to come in, so he just has me work on her computer and type the missing two paragraphs of text. I could've sworn I typed all of the text she gave me, in fact, the paper in which the paragraphs are written is not even the same paper as the text I already wrote on Friday, but whatever. I can't compare them either, because Neil says he doesn't know where the other papers are. I don't know, I guess with my first day nervousness I missed it. When I finish I place it on the server so that Larry can redo the design. I don't do anything else other than get lunch for everyone at around one. After we eat Neil, Larry and Carol, go back to work on the brochure. As they talk fonts, elements and placement, I'm left on my own. I wait a bit for Neil to notice that I'm not needed, hoping he'll tell me I can leave. But he makes no such notion, and I feel like I'm supposed to do something. I decide to go to my office and hang for ten or fifteen minutes and then if no one needs me I'll ask if I can leave. But just as I turn to go Neil calls me.

"Would you mind checking the photo archives for a picture of a giraffe and another of a cool texture background?" He asks without looking up from the computer screen. "You know how to check it, right?"

"I... uh, haven't been shown how to work the archive..." I stammer, feeling stupid. He looks up and gives me a blank look. "But I think I could figure it out." I add quickly, feeling like I should know how to do this. I turn on the computer that houses the photo archive, and it takes me a couple of minutes to find it in the hard drive. The archive opens and there are hundreds of lists on it. I have no idea how to search for what I need. I try some logic and look for a search button. Eureka! Okay I type giraffe, and about twenty different ones come up. I pick three of them and save them on the desk top.

The textured background proves to be more challenging as five long lists come up. When Larry walks by on his way to the printer, I take the opportunity to ask him if there's any particular background they need. He tells me to get something that goes with canned corn. The brochure is for a prestigious canned vegetable corporation, that only deals in organic vegetables. I don't see how a giraffe ties in to the whole concept, but hey, right now I just need to concentrate on finding this corn related background.

When I finally get home, I'm surprised that it's only three o'clock. Since it's such a nice day outside I decide to go to the beach. It's so relaxing to just be able to lay here and forget about the day. I don't know how long I'm out before Courtney and Lydia set their towels next to mine under the umbrella. They bring drinks and snacks and we munch while I tell them about my day.

"So what background did you end up with?" Lydia asks half interested as she watches a group of guys playing volleyball.

"Well I found three that I thought appropriate for the subject, but apparently they weren't. Neil just searched himself and got one with purplish clouds."

"How does that relate to vegetables?" Courtney asks raising an eyebrow.

I shrug, and take some pretzels. I go on telling them how I actually designed my own version of the vegetable brochure. After the database search, Neil didn't show any signs that I should go home, so I went back to my office and played with Photoshop to kill some time. Next thing I knew I had a whole new design for the brochure. I almost showed Larry and Neil, to see what they thought, but just when I was about to, Jim said Neil was done with the proof and that he was really pleased with it. So I just threw it in my drawer and then mustered enough courage to ask if it was okay that I went home. While I was in my office Carol had left, so I thought it would be alright if I left also.

"We're we going tonight, anyway?" I ask, trying to change the subject.

"I was thinking downtown?" Courtney says looking at Lydia and then at me.

"Sure, I can do downtown." I answer, "Actually Ivan said he had to go to the office, because they have a big case they need to finish for tomorrow. Maybe when they're done he can meet us-"

"It's girl's night out, you know..." Lydia says annoyed.

"Yeah, look, forget about Ivan. Let's just have a good time, should we?" Courtney pleads, and shakes her head.

"Alright, alright, forget I said anything." I have to remind myself sometimes that being single bears a whole different state of mind. I know they want to go and have a good time, and not have to drag a couple around. I guess I need some friend time anyway, I forget how much fun we used to have just us girls.

Eight

We walk into the Eight Ball bar at about eleven at night. It's the third bar we've been to so far and I'm already a little buzzed from the Apple Martinis I've been sipping. Lydia and I go to the ladies room while Courtney and Rosie go to the bar. After about ten minutes standing in line, we finally make it back to the bar. To my surprise I not only find another Apple Martini waiting for me, but a very solemn looking Courtney and a smiling Ivan are at the bar as well.

"Ivan?" I really didn't expect him, but I get a feeling Courtney thinks I called him. "What a surprise!"

"Yes, a wonderful surprise it is!" Courtney coils over obnoxiously.

I don't know if it's my imagination, or Courtney's insufferable tone, but Ivan seems a little uncomfortable. He quickly goes on to explain that when they were done with work, one of his coworkers suggested going to get something to drink to unwind after such a busy day. He points to their table where there are six or seven people, but the one person that catches my attention is Eve, the receptionist. She's the only girl, and non-lawyer of the group; she's quite chummy talking to the guy next to her, whom I think is another newbie at the firm, Robert or something.

Ivan excuses himself quickly, I guess partly because of my friends' annoyed glares, and to get back to his table, where there's a lively conversation. He gives me a peck on my forehead, and promises to call tomorrow. I'm relieved when Lydia says that it's obvious I didn't call him to meet us here, but at the same time that gives me an uneasy feeling. I shake it off and drink my martini in a couple of sips. I don't get much resistance when I suggest moving on the next bar. As we walk out, I take one last glance towards Ivan's table to see if he sees me leave. I try to wave to him, but he's deep in conversation with Eve and Robert so he doesn't see me.

The rest of the night is sort of blurry, I blame the Martinis, but deep down I know it's something else. We don't stay out overly late since tomorrow is Monday, but by the time we get home I'm exhausted. Courtney, however, insists on making eggs and bacon and I realize that actually I am a little hungry.

"What's up with that girl, Eve?" Courtney asks me casually as she eats the last bite of egg.

"What do you mean?" I know just what she means, but don't want to talk about it.

"Well, I don't know… I mean why was she there?"

"It's the people he works with, I didn't find it abnormal. Sure I know he's always working, and we hardly see each other, but I have to trust him, don't I?"

"I don't know, Sara." Courtney shakes her head. "Sometimes I think he doesn't deserve you."

I sigh and bring my plate to the sink. Not wanting to continue with this I tell her that I'm tired and go to my room. I know she's just looking out for me, but I already have told myself all this same stuff. I just don't want to dwell on it. Lying awake in bed I go through the events of the evening. If Eve was acting in any particular way, I didn't notice, then again she always has that smug look about her. I'm just reading too much into it. I stop worrying about it and focus on sleep so I can be rested for work tomorrow.

A few short hours later I'm back at my new job, learning more about my responsibilities. I decide to make a list because there are a lot of things that need to be done throughout the day and I don't want to forget anything important. Keeping the printer trays full, the toner in check and making sure the supply shelves are stocked with blank CD's and the like, are just a few of my duties. I know these sound menial, but eventually I'll move up and get into more of the design aspect of the job.

As I fill one of the printer trays with laser paper, I'm startled by a voice behind me. "Sara..." It's Neil, twirling his glasses on one hand, as he often does. "Would you mind going to the bistro across the street and picking up some lunch?"

"I... sure, you need me to go right away?" I ask looking at my watch. Twelve forty three.

"Um yes, if you could, we usually eat at one. Amy will give you the list with the orders." With that he smiles and goes back to his office. I actually don't have anymore than a couple of dollars in change, and was counting on using the lunch card Ms. Stork/Stark gave me to use in the cafeteria downstairs. It runs a tab and takes the balance out of your check and it also gives a discount, which I thought could come in handy. I hope I have enough time to get something when I come back from the bistro.

When Amy gave me everyone's money for their food with the order list I counted a hundred dollars and thought it was a little much for lunch, but that's about how much it costs at this place. Apparently it's quite exclusive and the food has to be good being that I had to wait almost half an hour for it to be made. Balancing a bunch of bags as I get back into the building I realize I won't be able to go to the cafeteria carrying all this. Besides, the forty-five minute lunch break is just about over. I make a mental note to stop by the vending machine at the upstairs cafeteria. I recall seeing some granola bars in there.

It's a few minutes after one thirty when I get back and everyone is already in the conference room waiting for their food.

I sit with them for a few minutes as I finish my Healthy Grain Granola Bar and they eat their bistro lunches.

"Are you sure you have enough with that?" Amy asks eyeing the granola.

"Oh, yes… I, uh, had a big breakfast." I smile trying not to look at her Mediterranean Dijon premium roasted ham baguette sandwich. I get up from the table with the real excuse that my lunch time is up. I make another stop by the vending machine on my way to my office and get some potato chips. Two bags. Plus some peanuts. I'd get a candy bar as well, except I ran out of change.

A couple of hours later I'm typing some more text for Amy when Larry knocks on the doorway's wall.

"Hey, Sara." He says holding out a folder towards me. "Here are some pictures, if you could scan them for me that'd be great."

"Sure, no problem… do you need them right away?" I ask hoping he doesn't. Luckily he tells me that tomorrow afternoon is fine.

He starts to walk out but turns back to face me again. "Hey, I know it's kind of a pain to have to get lunch for everyone… I had to do it myself until I got promoted."

"You were a Junior too?" I ask happy to know that I now have definite affirmation that this position is only temporary.

"Yeah, I was one of them, and I stuck it out." He tells me and then quickly adds, "Listen, about the lunch thing… it won't be daily, but almost. So what I did is bring something from home and occasionally splurge on the bistro lunches, otherwise it's almost impossible to get something downstairs and have enough time to eat."

"So, were a lot of you guys juniors at one time?" I ask, not picturing Neil as anything below senior status.

"Well… let's just say there have been many Juniors that came through here, but I'm the only one that made it passed the first few months." He tells me sheepishly. "Maybe you will too, I think you're doing pretty good so far."

"Thanks." I say, unsure if he means that the previous Juniors didn't make it because they didn't like the job, or because they were terrible at it. Being so new here, I did not want to ask. "And thanks for the advice with lunch."

I end up going to pick up lunch everyday this week except Thursday. Since I only have about five to ten minutes left to eat on the days I go to pick food up, I've been taking things like nuts or carrot sticks that I can eat quickly. Then at break time in the afternoon I'll try and eat a sandwich that I keep in a little lunch bag in my closet. On Thursday, though, I took advantage of my free lunch time and splurged in the cafeteria. I even ate outside by the picnic tables they have on the third floor terrace.

Today, Friday, we have a meeting about the Nu-Vegetables account and Neil wants to make it a 'lunch meeting'. This means that the company buys lunch and we get to talk about work while we eat. Of course, meetings like these warrant non-cafeteria food, so I'm in charge of going to the Illead Gourmet Bistro and getting some very fabulous food. Although, since the meeting doesn't start until the food arrives, I get to eat within a nice and long time frame because these meetings can go on for a while. Neil wants to go over the brochure and present the final proof, he also wants to share how he worked and designed it; sort of a 'tips and tricks' session as Amy calls it.

It takes me roughly 35 minutes to get the lunch. Everything is cooked to order, and because of the nature of this type of food, they don't take phone pre-orders. They cook as you order, from scratch and admittedly it smells divine. The food is so good that not a sound can be heard while we eat except that of forks clicking and Neil talking. A short while later the table gets cleared and the meeting continues in full swing. Neil's brochure looks quite good, the backgrounds of the purple clouds and the giraffe are seamlessly integrated and blended. I'm impressed how they actually work out so well into the design without looking weird. There's even an element to the design that almost looks familiar, but innovative at the same time.

The meeting goes on for about two hours; Neil goes over how he designed the brochure, and also the account itself. Apparently if they like this brochure they will turn all their advertising needs to us. Everyone is ecstatic about this, since Nu-Vegetables is such an important company, and doing all their advertising would be a great gain for Tivoli & Parks. Before we wrap the meeting up Neil says he has some other things to go over. He opens up his planner and hums to himself a bit before he starts to speak.

"Okay…" he starts, "like most of you know, the International Advertising World Conference is taking place in about a week.

Usually myself, Amy or Dave attend it, or if we're busy the next person down the line goes. Well... being that we're anticipating the Nu-Vegetable account, we're going to be extremely busy and we don't think any of us can make it. However, we believe that our presence in this Conferences is very important, so we have thought it over and we'd like to have Sara attend it for us."

What?? Did I hear right? I'm attending a conference by myself, representing a company I've barely just begun to work for?

"Of course, it's in the Virgin Islands this year, so you should get your passport in order if you don't have it already."

The Virgin Islands?? Hmmm... the Virgin Islands, well, that doesn't sound half bad. But wait! I can't go, I mean...

"So be ready to go a week from Sunday, Marcia will have your itinerary ready and everything you'll need. Amy and I will also need to go over what's expected of you during the trip. But we'll be talking about that later next week."

A dumbfounded nod is all I can answer right now, while I recuperate from this little surprise. I don't hear much of the last minutes of the meeting, I hope nothing important was said. The more I think about it, though, the more I feel this trip will be exciting. It's also my first business trip, and that alone makes it worthwhile.

I spend the rest of the afternoon writing up text for Amy and daydreaming about the Virgin Islands. In between writing I sneak a few Internet peeks to find out information on the International Advertising World Conference, and on the Virgin Islands. Before

I know it it's almost seven and nearly everyone has gone home. David, who's a Senior Graphic Designer, is the last one in the office, I'm a little annoyed that he didn't let me know ahead of time like most of the others do so I'd get a head start on shutting things off.

"So, they're sending you, eh?" He says as he perches over the doorway with a smirk. "I hope you can handle it being so new to the job and all."

"I don't have much choice, do I?" I answer him with a forced snicker. I don't know why, but he sounds a little put off or something. It's not like I asked to go, but if you ask me, it's better for them to send someone who's not very needed now that they will be so busy with the Nu-Vegetable account. It would be great to be involved in the designing of this huge account for the learning experience; but I have to admit that going on this trip does sound exciting. It also affirms that they must think I'm doing a good job, doesn't it?

Nine

"Courtney says you're leaving tomorrow, lucky dog!" Lydia says as she sets camp next to me on the beach. "I can't believe they asked you to go, that's so cool."

Actually, now that I think about it I realize that they never really asked; they basically just told me I was going.

"Ah, who cares, the important thing is that you're going!" She says when I tell her this minor fact. "I wish my boss would send me off to the Caribbean somewhere."

"You are your boss." I frown at her.

"Yeah, right." She slaps her knee.

"Hey aren't those the Volleyball Guys from the other day?" Courtney points towards a group of guys walking towards the volleyball net.

"They sure are!" Lydia says practically salivating. "Check out the dark haired one with the great behind..." That describes about half the guys – the other half are lean just with lighter hair - but I can see the one she's staring at, and he is actually quite hot. Apparently he notices her staring and waves before he runs off with the others to start a game. I lay face down on my towel while my two friends watch the game and cheer the guys on.

I don't know how long I've been out, but Lydia's loud laughter wakes me up. When I sit up and find that we are surrounded by a bunch of guys. It takes me a minute to realize that half the volleyball team is with us. I feel a little embarrassed as I straighten up and rub my face; Surely I must be quite a sight after having slept for who knows how long with my face buried into the towel.

"Looks like your friend's awake." The dark haired guy Lydia was ogling over says as he notices me.

"Hey Sara, this is Mikalo, he's from Brazil." She's absolutely mesmerized by this guy.

"Nice to meet you." He says as I detect a definite accent now that I'm fully awake.

"And this is Rob, Biel and Santiago." Courtney says pointing to each guy respectively. I can never remember names when I'm introduced to people, but I manage to remember one of them, or almost anyway.

"Beille... Bail... how do you say it again?" I ask looking at the guy whose name caught me.

"It's Biel, B-i-e-l, pronounced 'Bee-el'." Courtney answers for him. "He's from Spain."

"Really? Nice to meet you Biel." I say.

"Santiago is also from Spain, they work together and their company sent them here for a few months. Rob here, is from good ole' Texas." Courtney adds with a smile.

"I've never been to Spain, but I hear it's beautiful there." I tell Biel, trying to make casual conversation. Truth is, I love Spain and I've been wanting to visit for the longest time.

"You should visit some time." Santiago says.

"Where in Spain are you guys from?" I ask them.

"I'm from Barcelona, and Santi's from Galicia." Biel answers.

We all sit and talk for a while, until it gets dark. I almost forgot that Ivan was supposed to call at around six or seven to go to dinner and a movie. I check my cell phone but there are no messages, so I assume he must have called the home phone. I don't know why he does that when he knows I have my mobile with me all the time. Oh, well I guess he doesn't want to bug me when I'm out having fun. He went into the office again today, but said he didn't think he'd stay too late.

The girls make plans to meet the volleyball guys – that's what they're called now – and call Rosie to meet them downtown. "See you girls later, then." Rob says waving as he makes his way towards the beach parking lot.

"Are you sure you can't come?" Biel asks as he and Santi also go towards their car.

"Yeah… I can't, I already made plans." I answer him hoping he won't ask what my plans are. "I'll see you guys at the beach again, I'm sure." I add not sure of what to say, and feeling a little stupid. They walk away as Courtney and Lydia stare after them. We then make our way back to the apartment.

The first thing I do is check the answering machine to see if Ivan called. His voice sounds crackly on the message, as if the cell is breaking up, but I can clearly hear that he can make an early dinner. He can't make the movies, however, because he's got a ton of work to do. He also says he'll understand if I want to take a rain check and go another night since he's limited with time. I immediately call him back and tell him that I'm game; if I don't see him tonight, I probably won't see him for like a week. I was hoping to spend the night over at his place, or better yet, have him stay over at mine since he hasn't even seen it yet. I know he has to work, but I'll try and persuade him anyway.

An hour later we're eating dinner at Magno's, my favorite Steak House, it's rather early so I'm not very hungry yet. I still order a steak and mashed potatoes, which I'm not even halfway done when Ivan has finished his own already.

"You don't want dessert, do you"? He asks rather eagerly. I understand he's under pressure to finish his current case at the firm, but I can't help feeling sort of rushed here and as if he rather be somewhere else.

I don't feel like swallowing a piece of chocolate cake whole, so I decline on the dessert, as well as on the coffee. He pays for dinner and we're off. On the way to my place I contemplate on asking him to stay, but think better of it. He talks about how much work he has to get done before Monday during the whole drive, so it's pointless to ask.

After a peck on the lips, a few words of apologetic excuses and a promise of a real night out with a stay over real soon, he speeds away. Feeling put off and frankly kind of lonely, I go change my clothes and call Courtney on her cell. "Where are you guys?" I ask as she greets me loudly amid lots of background noise. I tell her of my ridiculous evening out with Ivan, and before long I'm making my way down to the Galleria to meet her at the Mist Bar. When I get there I meet Courtney by the entrance and she leads me to a table somewhere in the middle of the bar. I find myself glad to see the 'volleyball guys' there as well as the girls.

It's been a while since I had fun with a group of guys without Ivan there. It's actually very refreshing. Before I can even get a waitress' attention an apple martini finds its way in front of me at the table. When I look questioningly at Courtney, she shrugs and points over to the guys. They all raise their glasses and we make a toast. I notice Lydia with Mikalo and wonder if it will turn into something this time or if it's just another week long relationship. After a second martini I find myself talking to Santiago about the 'Running with the Bulls' in Pamplona. He's been there a couple of times and the whole thing sounds nuts, but at the same time quite exhilarating.

A couple of hours later my radar is sending me some very loud signals from Santi. Although I know I can't, I also think that he's more into a good time than a relationship, so I try to sustain myself. With the buzz I've got going, though, I'm finding it quite hard to keep from throwing my arms around him as we dance to a fast beat song and laugh about I don't know what. Right next to us is Rosie and she's quite content dancing with Rob, while Lydia and Mikalo sit at a table in the corner well into a heavy make out session.

"Want another drink?" Santi asks as he wipes a droplet of sweat from his forehead.

Feeling wobbly and slightly nauseous I start to head towards the bar. "I think some water will be good!" We find Courtney and Biel conversing over a glass of wine each. Courtney gives me a sideways glance as I sit next to her.

"What gives? You two seem pretty chummy…" She whispers towards my ear. "Did something happen with Ivan? This is very unlike you."

The bartender hands me a tall glass of water and I sit down to prevent a potential floor crash landing. "I know… I really haven't done anything, I mean yet, or I won't. Really. But, you know, he's cute and nice. But I know he wants one thing, not interested in a girlfriend. But nothing wrong with having fun, you know? I definitely won't do more than maybe a kiss, but probably not even that, I'm with Ivan, but I don't know if I am happy with him, I don't think so-"

"Just how many martinis did you have?" Courtney shakes her head amused. I just laugh and try to make sense of what I said, and just drink some more water. Some time later, or maybe just a few minutes, I'm on the outside terrace with Santi, he hands me another glass of water as I let the breeze hit my face while I hold the balcony rail for support. All I can do is hope I don't get sick, that would just be too embarrassing in front of this guy.

"How are you feeling? Okay?" He seems concerned.

"I'm fine thanks, just no more martinis please…"

He looks at me and smiles and for a second we're close enough to kiss. The next second we find ourselves actually kissing. It's a sweet kiss and when we part, even though I'm quite loaded, I feel a little awkward. I don't know what to make of it, and I hope I didn't send too many signals. Although I could easily spend the night with him, my conscience is still with me, even in my current state.

"I'm sorry, I usually don't do this… I hardly know you, and I think you're getting the wrong impression of me."

"Hey, no problem, it's okay. I didn't think you were the type for a quick, how you say… adventure?" He says as he moves from me a little. "I was hoping, of course and with the dancing and everything, maybe… but you know, I understand."

Shit. I wish I wasn't so damn conscientious and I would just take this guy home. But… I just can't. And I can't do this to Ivan either. I already feel horrible for having kissed another guy as it is. Just as I'm apologizing to Santi again, Courtney walks over eyeing us with suspicious anticipation. I'm sure she'd love having caught us in some passionate kiss or something. Hey a couple of minutes earlier and she would have. Well, maybe not a passionate kiss, but whatever.

"We're about ready to leave," She says and then smirks. "Are you coming with us or are you...?" She points at Santi and me back and forth.

Embarrassed I tell her that I'm going with her, wobbling a little when I let go of the rail. We all walk back inside to meet Rosie and Lydia who are by the bar with Rob. We say goodbye at the parking lot and agree to meet at the beach tomorrow if it's a nice day. As we walk to our cars I take one last look back and see Santi talking to Biel in front of their own car. He sees me looking and waves, I wave back and keep walking out.

Before heading home we stop at the Prix Diner for some early breakfast. Sobering up after a few cups of coffee, I cringe at the thought of my kiss with Santi.

"I think it's your conscience telling you that something is wrong with your present relationship." Lydia says after hearing the story.

Not wanting to get into it about Ivan at these hours, I quickly change the subject. "Hey, speaking of relationships, is that what we might see happening with you and Mikalo?"

"Yeah, you two were on overdrive all night, and you're here with us now." Courtney says raising an eyebrow. "This can only mean that its not about a fly-by screw."

Lydia blushes, something rarely seen, as she smiles. "We'll see... He's really different and I just feel great when I'm with him."

"Oh shut up!" Rosie slams her napkin down on her lap. "Love sucks. Specially when it always manages to happen to others."

"What, you spent half the night dancing with Rob, didn't you?" I tell her as I recall seeing her before the martinis kicked in.

"Yeah well, it was just dancing, there were like no special sparks or any of that shit." Rosie shakes her head and takes a huge bite of her English Muffin.

I know Rosie is exaggerating, well at least a little, but her words sort of hit a soft spot with me. I can't really remember the last time I felt 'special sparks' with Ivan. Well, honestly I can't remember any special anything, since I don't ever see him anymore. When I am with him it's like he's always in a hurry to be somewhere else.

Ten

"How about going to the movies?" Courtney asks as she steps out into the balcony. It's almost five in the afternoon and it hasn't stopped raining. I've been sitting out here on the terrace watching the rain and the ocean.

"What's playing?" I ask her as I think to myself how cozy I am just sitting here relaxing. I guess, however, that getting out for a while wouldn't be a bad idea. It's been such a lazy day, both Courtney and I slept in late. Lulled by the sound of the rain I didn't see any reason to get out of bed. Besides, the memories of last night have left me with a bit of shame and I'm glad for the rain keeping us from the beach and from seeing the volleyball guys.

We decide on a suspense movie and head for the theater. After the movie we stop at the Prix Diner for some dinner and not before long our conversation sways towards last night's events.

"So you really don't like Santi?" Courtney presses.

"I'm with Ivan, Court and even if I wasn't, Santi isn't my type." I go on telling her how he's just a one fling guy and I'm not into that.

"That's bullshit!" She says, almost offended. "He just hasn't found the right woman, that's all."

"I think he finds the right woman at least once a week." I tell her sneering. To no avail, Courtney tries to convince me that Santi can be changed. In the end, the realization that tomorrow is already Monday takes over and I just nod along with her and just agree that Santi can be turned into a faithful loving boyfriend.

The next morning I arrive at work at my usual seven thirty to turn all the machines on, but Neil is already there. He blurts a good morning after what I perceive to be a sideways glare at my clothes. I shrug it off, taking it as a normal Neil reaction, until I notice Marcia also looking at my clothes in a peculiar way, her glare being a lot more exaggerated. It isn't after half the staff comes in that I notice everyone is wearing suits, something not usually seen here were they always wear business casual. It all makes sense when Amy approaches me and takes me aside to ask me why I am not dressed up. When I give her a blank stare she 'reminds' me that today Mr. Tivoli and his son are coming around make their 'Walk Around' the office'.

"I'm sure I told you on Friday to come in a suit today." She says slightly irritated. "This is really important to Neil, he wants to make our department look good and stand out." She sighs and purses her lips.

"I'm sorry, but I really don't recall that you mentioned anything, are you sure you-" I start to say.

"Alright listen, it doesn't matter right now, you should just know that about every second Monday of the month is 'Walk Around' day." She tells me as if I should've known this from my first day. I'm about to say something when Neil walks over and asks Amy how come I wasn't aware and to make sure I'm covered on the issue.

I'm standing there feeling a little awkward being talked about as if I'm not there. I'm about to say that I wasn't told about this again, when Neil suddenly turns to me as if I've just materialized.

"Is there any way you can run home to change and be back in less than half hour?" He's so serious about this whole thing, you'd think his job was on the line.

"Well... sure, I'll try."

"Just be back in a half hour." With that he abruptly turns and walks towards his office.

"Common! Go, go, go!" Amy leads me by my arm towards the exit.

Riding down the elevator I realize that I don't own any suits. I think about borrowing something from one of the girls but they're all working or live too far away. The Gap doesn't have any suits, so visiting Courtney is out. My only solution is to go into one of the shops here in downtown and spend half a week's salary on a suit.

I walk into the first women's clothing store I see. Luckily, there's a SALE sign on the window.

"Could you show me where the sale items are?" I ask the sales lady. She gives me a puckered look before she leads me to a rack way in the back of the store.

I quickly search through and find three suits my size. One is hot pink with thick green stripes and bright yellow furry trim. Well, that actually leaves me with two suits; a light blue linen one, which is great except for the brownish stain on the upper left side of the skirt. And a mustard yellow pantsuit, which is surprisingly very nice, except for the three hundred and fifty nine dollar price tag. And that's the sale price. This pretty much leaves me with no other choice but the stained one. I try it on and apparently the stain is pretty well hidden by the jacket, so as long as the jacket is on no one should see it.

I ask the sales woman if she could reduce the price a little more because of the stain.

"I can reduce it by fifteen dollars but no more than that. These are designed in France and are meticulously tailored, I can't let it go for less." She says in a sour tone after much huffing and eye rolling. Truth is, the women that shop in this store would not give a cent to buy a stained outfit, even if it was designed on top of the Eiffel Tower. She can be glad to get rid of the thing and make money on it to boot.

The final price still sets me back quite a bit, but considering the circumstances I don't have much of a choice. As I sprint back to the office I realize that this is the first time that I've gone clothes shopping and not felt any joy in it. I make it back just barely over a half hour only to be greeted by a glaring Neil and a sneering Marcia.

"You haven't changed yet? What where you doing? They'll be here any second!" Neil sounds exasperated.

"I went to get something down the street." I point to my shopping bag. "It'll just take me a minute to change into it." I don't wait for an answer and just march right back to my closet. The bathroom is on the other side of the reception area so going to my closet gets me out of sight faster. I should be able to change there.

I'm trying to pull my new skirt on as I kneel behind the desk, not having a door can really prove to be a pain. I almost have it on when I hear someone by the entrance in the hallway.

"Sara, you need to come to the conference room, Mr. Tivoli Senior and Junior are here for the 'Walk Around' everyone is over there already." Larry is standing by the doorway trying to see what I'm doing behind the desk. "Uh, are you all right?"

"Yes, I'll be right there… I just need to get something." This is beyond embarrassing. I hope he can't tell that I'm getting dressed back here. "Go ahead, I'm right behind you." I smile awkwardly.

He doesn't look very convinced. "Alright, hurry up though, Neil gets a little touchy with these 'Walk Arounds'."

Neil is giving a speech as I sneak into the conference room. Everyone's standing so it's easy to just walk right in unnoticed. "So as you can see we're working double hard to make sure the Nu-Vegetable account gets the best quality design campaign we can manage." With this Neil finishes up and everyone starts to disperse back into their offices. Mr. Tivoli Sr. nods and starts to make his way out as Neil approaches Mr. Tivoli Jr. He starts to talk to him in a low voice and then invites him into his office.

As I'm making my way back to my own closet, Amy approaches me and asks me to come by her office maybe sometime tomorrow so we can go over the trip next week. She says she has a lot to go over with me before I leave. I'm pretty nervous about going to The Virgin Islands by myself, it would definitely be nice if Ivan could come too. But I know that's impossible with his job, he actually had mentioned that he'd be working late pretty much every day this week.

Later in the evening as Courtney and I watch TV, I'm surprised to get a call from Ivan. He says he just got home and wanted to check in. He sounds so sweet I almost want to jump in my car and go over his place. If I wasn't so tired I would. He wants to do something next Sunday when he'll have some time off, apparently he forgot about my trip.

"I can't... I'm leaving on my trip for work on Sunday, remember?"

"That's right, damn I forgot about that. I'm sorry, I've just been so swamped with work and all..." He says apologetically.

"Hey, perhaps we can do something before you leave? Some lunch maybe?"

"That sounds nice, I'd love to see you." Then in a lower voice I add, "I really miss you."

"Me too, sweets. But I'll see you soon." He sounds a little down. I hope that means he realizes that we do need to start spending more time together. We say good night and I go to bed thinking about him. I make up my mind to go see him tomorrow after work at his office. I'll get us some nice take-out dinner, maybe something from the expensive deli I pick up lunch from for the guys at work. That'll be nice. I might even convince him to come spend the night at my place, so he can finally see the new apartment.

The next day, I find myself dragging through the afternoon. It seems like the end of the day is farther away than the end of time itself. Once nearly everyone is gone I start to shut things off, hoping that no one will need to use the wax machine or the black and white laser printers. I leave the color laser for last since that is the one mostly used. Luckily Neil had to leave early today, so I won't run the risk of him finding out that I'm turning things off before the last person leaves.

I'm finally on my way to the deli at twenty after seven. They close at seven thirty so the two girls on the counter aren't very happy to see me. When I ask for the Lobster Platter they are practically growling, but the owner happens to be there and he knows I come in frequently with large orders for the office. He 'happily' complies and the two girls silently walk to the back to prepare my order.

Half an hour later, I'm in the elevator of Ivan's office building. I get off on his floor and walk towards the reception desk. The computer is on, but no one's in the chair. I call Ivan's name as I make my way towards his office. His door is closed so I knock a couple of times.

"Now, now, my little red hot sex machine, you don't have to knock... come in and eat me my slave!" Wow, I guess he misses me too. I was hoping to eat the lobster, actually, then get together at my place later. I mean sex on his desk is not exactly my idea of romantic. I guess he's been working way too much. He's probably just kidding. I open the door, and the room is dark with the blinds closed and a small candle on Ivan's desk.

"What took you so long? Common baby, come and get me, I'm all ready for you!" I gasp when I find him naked on his desk spread eagle with a huge dollop of whipped cream over his privates.

"Ivan!" I switch the light on.

"SARA!!" His eyes are just about popping out as he struggles to get off the desk wiping his privates off with a shirt that's lying on his chair.

"Yes master, I—" a familiar voice comes from the hallway. I'm speechless as I find out the voice belongs to Eve, as she enters the room wearing nothing but two mini pink post it notes over her boobs, and a bunch of grapes over her front.

"Ivan, darling, why the hell is she here?" Eve says glaring at me.

All Ivan can do is stare from me to her.

I don't know how long it takes me to register what is happening. But I manage to pick my feet up and start to make my way out.

"You dropped your post its, slut." I tell Eve as I walk passed her. She gasps looking at her naked chest and starts to say something but I just run off to the elevators.

Eleven

When I walk into the apartment, I notice I'm still holding the bag with the damn Lobster Platter I got for me and that bastard.

Asshole.

I toss the bag onto the kitchen table and collapse on the couch. I turn on the TV, but just stare at it not really watching. I don't know how long I'm sitting there looking at the screen when Courtney walks in.

"What are you watching?" She asks as some figures painted in blue and purple dance to some weird music on the Culture TV channel. I try to answer her but I can't get any words out.

"Sara? Hello? Yoo-hoo!" She sits next to me and waves a hand over my eyes. As she brings me back to reality I suddenly lose control and break down, shamelessly sobbing on her shoulder.

"Sweetie, what's wrong? What happened?" She asks patting my back and handing me a tissue, "What happened?" She asks again as I look up at her blowing my nose and spill the whole thing, detail by nasty detail.

"I'm such an idiot, Court," I tell her slapping my forehead. "I'm a moron, an absolute moron, I should've seen it, hell I should've listened to you when you kept saying I deserve better."

"Don't Sara, don't blame yourself," Court says to me firmly, "the guy's an obvious slime, he knew what he had, but he couldn't pass the chance to screw some cheap, easy sleaze, I mean… Post it notes?" Although I feel like shit, this makes me laugh out loud.

"Did you say you still have that Lobster dinner?" Courtney asks sneering.

I feel better after talking to Courtney. I don't know what I'd do without her. We both eat like pigs and finish every bite of the lobster.

I try to keep busy until I leave for the Virgin Islands. I think some time away will do me good, although I'm growing more and more apprehensive as Sunday nears. On Thursday Amy goes over what's expected of me and every thing I should be doing during my trip. She keeps coming with more things to add to my list like every hour after that. I guess she wants to make sure I'm well prepared, but it gets a little annoying.

Neil also stops by my closet and tells me to gather as much information as possible from the speeches and all the people I'll be talking to. He also wants me to make sure to tell everyone how Tivoli-Parks has acquired the Nu-Vegetable account and how huge that is. Of course he also wants me to not say too much to the wrong people. Since I'm not familiar with who is who in the advertising world, as he puts it, Neil gives me a list of which persons are okay to talk to, which are not, which are alright for small talk and the ones to avoid all together no matter what.

When Sunday finally arrives, I'm starting to feel a little nervous. Then, in the middle of packing I'm taken aback when the phone rings and the caller ID flashes Ivan's number. Court grabs the phone from my hand and throws it on the bed, then orders me to keep packing.

"I don't even want to hear that you called him from the Virgin Islands." She's saying. "Promise me. Okay?"

I look at her and sigh. "Yes, I promise." I hope I'll be busy enough not to even think about him at all.

The captain says that the flight from Ft. Lauderdale to St. Croix will be about three hours and with a full plane, I'm glad it's not more than that. I'm stuck in the middle seat and I just hope I can wait until we land to go to the bathroom, because it will be impossible to get out of the seat without practically climbing on my neighbor's lap. A while later, when the flight attendant comes out with the drink carriage I peek into the First Class cabin as she opens the curtain to see where I almost had the chance of sitting.

I say almost because when I approached the ticket counter before my flight, the lady checking me in kept clicking the computer keys and telling me to please wait a minute while she looks something up. "What do you suppose this means?" She asked her co-worker on the next station. He looked over and then a look of recognition swept over him.

"That means there has been a class status change." He explains to her, as if I'm not standing there. "This ticket was originally First Class for someone else, it was purchased by a company for an Amy Brown... then they transferred it to a Sara Livingston and downgraded it to coach."

At this point I just wanted my boarding pass so I could be on my way and disappear, but she still has to inform me that since Tivoli-Parks paid for the ticket, I couldn't upgrade back to first class by paying for it myself. Then she had to measure my carry on and call someone to verify if a half inch over the limit was okay. When I finally was able to walk to the gate I strode off trying to ignore the glares from the people in the long line.

The flight attendant is now by my row with the drink trolley and I ask for some water. I get comfortable, or as comfortable as I can get sandwiched between two people in my narrow seat, and start to read a magazine. As the flight attendant goes back through the curtain, I get another peek into First Class, this time I see a good looking man in his wide leather seat sipping champagne as he's offered some canapés from a silver tray. I want to say he looks familiar, but I just shrug it off and go back to my magazine.

The hotel is magnificent. It's tropical but very upscale, the lobby is huge and filled with majestic palm trees. Then there are sets of luxurious dark brown leather couches scattered all around, each with it's own dark wood and rattan side table and matching coffee table for each set. The ceiling is very high, it goes about three floors up, where you can see the balconied hallways leading to the rooms in the first three floors. The hotel itself looks to be about fifteen floors high. To the left there are these huge French windows through which you can see a lush garden with a pool that surrounds the hotel all around. Then, looking through the pretty garden there's a beautiful turquoise ocean.

I take my suitcases and proceed over to the polished marble registration counter. A smiling young woman greets me and starts to look in the computer as I tell her my name.

"I'm sorry, what company did you say you were with?" She asks as she looks up from the computer.

Great here we go again. "Tivoli-Parks."

"Mmmm, okay… I show an Amy Brown under Tivoli-Parks… you're here for the World Advertising International Convention, correct?" She keeps clicking on the computer and before I can answer her face lights up, "Oh, wait here you are! I couldn't see your name because you have been moved… It seems that someone else was supposed to be coming, and when they switched and booked in your name, they requested a different room for you."

She tells me that instead of the main hotel, I will be in the smaller guest rooms right next to the main building. It's just a five minute walk through the gardens. She prints out the paperwork, and she gets both copies, Amy's and mine, she puts Amy's aside and I manage to read a bit of it before she crumples it up. At the top I could just make out "Penthouse Room 415-416A".

I get a slight feeling of disappointment realizing that I have been 'downgraded' once again, getting only one of the smaller guest rooms. Oh well, hey I know that soon enough I'll be on my way to Amy's status, higher if I really work hard. I can't get ahead of myself, I mean I just started this job and I'm still on the low end of the scale. Let's face it, I'm lucky enough to be on this trip at all! Plus, I'm sure my little room costs a lot more than the best room in… let's say a Holiday Inn or something like that.

The girl hands me my receipt, keys, a map of the hotel as well as a folder with the name 'Tivoli-Parks' imprinted on the upper right corner. She explains how to find my room in the 'Surf' Building. Apparently there are three smaller guest buildings called 'Surf', 'Tortoise' and 'Shell'.

A doorman opens the French doors for me and I find myself in the great garden. I follow the brick path, as the counter girl instructed, while I take in the pretty flowers, palm trees and soft grass. I cross a small wooden bridge that goes over the pool and to the left is the 'Surf' building. I find my room, 213, after I take an elevator ride to the second floor of the three story building. The first thing I do is open the curtains and see that there isn't a balcony, but the view of the gardens below is quite nice, except for a huge palm tree that obstructs half the window. Oh well, I'll spend most of my time in the main hotel for the conference anyway, so that's alright.

After I unpack everything and settle myself, I take a look at what's inside the folder. There are the schedules for all events during the week, a list of all the companies present and what countries they are from. There are also brief descriptions of the featured speakers, and a bunch of other information pertaining to the conference. I take the lists I got from Neil and Amy and add them to the folder and it's then I realize that I forgot the list Neil made of the people I should and shouldn't talk to. Oh well, I really don't have much information anyway since I'm so new so I'll just keep it to light small talk with everyone. Looking over the schedule one more time I'm caught by surprise that there's a listing for Sunday evening, that's today! I thought the conference started tomorrow. I read it and it says it's an unofficial welcoming cocktail party; it starts at seven. Shit! I look at my watch and it's five after seven.

A while later I'm walking across the garden with my map trying to find the 'Breeze Room', a large ballroom on the east side of the main hotel somewhere. I'm now about a half hour late, but I figure no one will notice since it's an unofficial party and everyone will just be scattered around drinking cocktails. The notice said 'cocktail attire' which I'm not quite sure what it should be so I just slipped into a cute sundress I bought for the trip and some strappy high heels.

I find the 'Breeze Room' after reading a huge sign by the lobby that had an arrow pointing to the direction of the ballroom and the words 'International Advertising Conference'. As I push open the huge white door to the room, instead of the usual rumbling of hundreds of voices that I expected to hear, all is quiet. The people in the back all turn to look at me as I awkwardly try to merge in with them. Apparently someone is giving a speech in the front of the room and everyone is listening quietly.

When the speech is over everyone breaks up into groups and all the bars around the room start to get busy. I'm at one of the bars and as I grab my martini I turn to find a familiar face smiling widely holding a drink up to mine. I'm momentarily speechless as he's the last person I'd expect to find here. Santi just stands there smiling clicking his glass to mine and waiting for me to say something.

"Hi!" I say and not coming up with anything else I take a sip of my drink. He then kisses me on both cheeks, something I learned is a Spaniard custom.

"Hello! What a surprise!" He smiles.

I nudge my head. "So, not to sound cliché…, but what are you doing here?"

"Well, I imagine the same thing you are!" He smiles even wider. "Did you come by yourself?"

I explain to him how I came by default, since no one else in the office could make it. He then tells me that he's here for his company, which specializes in color laser printers and that they cater mostly to advertising agencies.

"I'm here with my colleague." He points left with his drink. "I think you know him —"

Just then Biel walks up also smiling and raising his eye brews at the sight of me with Santi.

"Hombre!" He exclaims, and then also proceeds to kiss me on both cheeks. I like this custom; it's so chic.

If I can forget the kissing incident with Santi the other night, this trip could turn out quite okay. I think hanging with these guys could be fun, they seem like good company. Definitely much better than being alone all week.

Santi and Biel tell me they work for 'Impri`Ma. S.A.', a Spanish company that has a couple of branch offices here in the States. One is in Ft. Lauderdale and the other in New York. They are engineers and come up with the prototypes and patents for color laser printers. I'm a little embarrassed to tell them of my entry level position, being that they are apparently quite successful. I fluff it up a bit and tell them I'm a Graphic Designer, leaving out the Junior, and that I mostly work on computer design. I leave out the fetching lunch and turning everything off at the end of the day bit also. And the typing part, the loading paper and ink part, getting coffee part… well, you get the picture. Anyway, I'll soon be a regular Graphic Designer anyway, so there's no need to tell them the measly details since they are temporary.

As I talk to them, I realize they are both wearing kakis and casual shirts, which makes me feel at ease about my own attire. That is until I realize that we're about the only ones that look casual, everyone else is wearing a suit and tie, the women are in elegant night dresses. Although when I mention this to them they just shrug..

"Hey, in Spain this is considered dressed up for a party." Biel says pointing at his clothes. "No one wears suits to parties that are not during work hours. You look great like that, most women in here look more like pheasants, with all that shiny on them."

I guess he has a point. We hang out together at the bar and order a few more drinks. They tell me about Spain, and how they got their jobs to come work here. Santi has been here for two years and Biel for one and a half, they both have contracts that expire at the end of the year. As the night goes by and a couple more drinks are ordered, I can't help but notice that both of them are quite good looking. I didn't notice before that Biel has deep green eyes, which set against his dark brown hair really stand out. He has high cheekbones and a straight nose with just a few freckles on an otherwise smooth complexion. Santi is also very handsome with blondish hair and blue eyes, he also has a firm square jaw that makes his face stand out.

I can't help but feel a little privileged to be sitting with these two. I notice a lot of women walk by and discreetly look at them; some of them glare at me as they continue to walk by. What I like most about them is their friendliness and how they don't even realize how good they look. They are just here having a good time and talking like old friends.

"Listen." Biel says as he puts a hand on my arm. "What are you doing tomorrow?"

"I guess whatever is on the schedule...?" I say, referring to the convention events. "Why?"

"Nah..." He takes a sip of rum and coke. "The daytime events are very boring, it's all sitting down conferences with long speeches. Nothing interesting. It's the evening events that count, and the parties after, when everyone is a little drunk... eh? See how it works?"

"Well, what will you guys be doing then?" I ask curious.

"Ah... the good part of these type of trips." Santi tells me winking. "We're going to explore the island, of course!"

"And you will come with us, no?" Biel asks me with an inviting smile.

"I guess I can't say no, can I?" I raise my drink and we toast to the occasion.

They walk me back to my room, something I insisted they need not do. I really didn't want them to know I'm at the 'small guest suites'. But they insisted saying that this is what they do and they cannot let me go to my room at night by myself. It's probably the drinks, but they don't really seem to notice or care that my room is in the 'poor' section. We make the plans for tomorrow and say goodnight.

As I walk into my room I can't help but be a little apprehensive about not being at the conference tomorrow. I hope I don't completely regret this when I wake up tomorrow on a more sober state. Still, these guys know about this conferences, so I should be okay... I mean the same people that are there during the day are also there at night, so I'll be able to talk to the ones on my list.

I really can't pass up a chance to visit this beautiful island, can I?

Twelve

I go up to Santi and Biel's room at around ten. I'm glad they are not early people either, apparently the Spanish schedule really agrees with me. I'm struck by the view they have from their balcony; it's just breathtaking. The room itself is splendid, they have white rattan furniture, two king beds each in a different room with a sliding partition, then there's a kitchen and a sitting TV room with a huge white linen couch. There are white flowing curtains on the windows and sliding door. The balcony is big enough for a large table and lounge chairs.

"Wow!" I can't help saying as Santi takes my bag and sets it down next to theirs by the kitchen. "What a room! Mine is so small and normal and my view is just of a big palm tree and part of the gardens…"

"Our company is very generous that way." Biel says as he prepares some stuff in the kitchen. Santi sits down on the white couch where his computer sits open on the coffee table.

"What would you like on your sandwich, Sara?" He asks me as I observe the ocean from the sliding door.

"Oh… anything, really, whatever you have." I say taken aback. "I didn't think to bring food… or I—"

"We are inviting you so you don't have to worry about anything." He smiles. "It's on us."

"Thanks… do you need help?" I ask walking towards the kitchen bar.

"No, no, no. I'm finished anyway." He shoos me away winking.

"Well, email is done, everyone has their answers back at the office, even the ones back in Spain. I can't believe they still email when I'm away." Santi stands up and walks towards the balcony. "I have printed some maps of the island, so we are ready to get lost!"

I follow him outside and take in the gorgeous day. The ocean is flat and there's a light warm breeze that feels wonderful. Biel finishes with the sandwiches and we pack it all up. A few minutes later we are on their rented jeep and off we go to explore the island. We start by driving up some mountains that are nearby the hotel. We go all the way to the top and check out the view, then we look for places that look good from up here to visit.

We make a tentative route that we agree to veer off if anyone of us finds something better along the way. We get back into the jeep, Biel driving, me on the passenger seat and Santi on the back seat were he can stand up and act goofy like he seems to like doing. Biel puts on a CD of U2 and we drive on. The sights are really beautiful, I've heard people say the Virgin Island are unbelievable, but it's nothing until you actually see it with your own eyes.

"Look at that beach down there!" I say as I see a secluded beach hidden below the mountain. I happen to see it by chance, otherwise it's easy to just drive on and never realize it's there. "We have to go and swim there you guys, look at it!"

Biel and Santi both look down towards the beach as it comes in and out of sight while we go along the turns of the mountain.

"Okay then, there we go!" We all scream together as the jeep makes its way towards paradise.

Once there the beach looks even better. The water is as clear as a pool's and the color is a turquoise blue. It's very shallow also and the sand is fine and white. There are a few rocks on both sides of the beach and palm trees scattered all around. It must be the most romantic location I've ever seen. We take out our towels and things from the jeep and set them on the beach under a palm tree. I sit down on my towel and take in the moment, Biel and Santi both sit down as well and we all just stare out to the ocean.

"Wow, this is the life, eh?" Biel says as he gives me a sideways glance. "Come on, let's go swim!" With that he yanks his shirt off and runs into the water as Santi follows. I take my time taking my shorts and shirt off, making sure my bathing suit is in place, then I apply some sunscreen all over and I head for the water.

We swim for a while and then Santi gets some masks and snorkels from the jeep and we go check out the coral beds nearby. It's like a different world underwater, the colors are so vibrant and it's full of beautiful tropical fish. I'm going along checking the coral and I'm startled by a huge dark round thing swimming underneath of me. I scream underwater and then look over at Biel who is nearby and I can see him laughing as bubbles stream out of his snorkel. He is pointing down and I look to see a huge turtle. I quickly follow it and manage to swim down to it and touch its shell I swim back up to catch my breath and notice the turtle going in circles around us. This is the coolest thing!

"That was incredible!" I yell over to Biel who's now a few feet away from me in the water.

A couple of hours later, starving from so much swimming we eat our sandwiches with intense gusto.

"What did you put in these sandwiches? They're so delicious." I ask Biel as I devour the thing.

"This is tomato bread, a Catalan specialty from Spain." He explains.

"Catalonia is in the northeast of Spain, right?" I've read about this before in a book my mother once gave me.

"I'm impressed! Most people have no idea what Catalonia is." Biel says.

"So this tomato bread, how do you make it?" I ask him, really wanting to know so I can make this for myself and Courtney back home.

"You cut a tomato in half and spread it all over the bread, then put some olive oil and a little salt on top. You can then put cheese, ham, or whatever you want in the middle to make a sandwich."

"Sounds easy enough, I could eat it every day for lunch!" I say taking the last bite of the 'tomato bread'.

As tempting as it is to stay on this beach we decide that we should continue on our discovery trip. We go up another mountain looking for some waterfalls that are marked on the map.

I'm lost in the beauty of my surroundings when Santi calls my name from the back seat.

"Uh… just out of curiosity, does Courtney have a boyfriend?" He asks me airily.

A little surprised at the question, I take a couple of seconds to respond. "No, she doesn't actually." I turn to him and frown. "Why?"

"Just wondering… she seems nice." He says as he sits back again and looks at the scenery go by.

We spend the rest of the afternoon driving around looking for the waterfalls and making many stops along the way. By five o'clock we decide it's time get back to the hotel so we have to give up the search for the waterfalls. The evening events start at seven and we're probably an hour from the hotel. The ride back is so relaxing; the sun is low on the horizon and warming our faces as we drive toward it.

I have a great feeling of wellbeing as the warm air hits my face while we cruise by an ocean side road. For a moment I forget I'm here for the advertising convention and feel like I'm on some dream vacation with two good friends. At the thought of returning to reality, my spirits dampen a bit. Soon it'll be back to listening to a bunch of advertising execs give uninteresting, long-winded speeches. Although, I have to admit that having someone to hang out with during all the convention activities really makes it so much better.

A couple of hours later we're back in the ballroom, this time it's the Sea Breeze Ballroom, a bit smaller and with lower lighting. The feel is less uptight than last night's and more like a typical cocktail party where people are relaxed and hanging out with friends. The atmosphere is more casual and there are no signs of speech podiums anywhere. I make the rounds with Biel and Santi as they introduce me to different people. I make sure to let them all know what company I represent, just as Amy and Neil instructed me to do, although I try not to say much as not to talk to the 'wrong' person from the list I lost.

While at the bar getting our second drink, we're approached by an important looking man who's smiling widely at Santi and Biel. He's about fifty, but with a youthful disposition and dressed up in beige linen.

"It's my favorite Spaniards!" He puts his drink down on the bar and pats both of them on the back.

"George, hombre! How you've been!" Santi grabs his extended hand and shakes it firmly. "We weren't sure if we'd see you here... glad you could make it."

"I know, I know, it's been crazy at the office. We had to fire our ad agency... Ahh, it was a mess... But here I am! Ready to relax and have some fun!" He takes out a box of cigars from his pocket and offers it to both guys. Biel notices me watching their exchange and with a soft hand on my shoulder turns me to face George.

"Sara this is a good friend of ours, George, George Halifax." Halifax... Halifax... this name should mean something to me...

"Nice to meet you, Mr. Halifax." We shake hands as Santi tells him I work for Tivoli-Barnes as a designer. I can't help feeling a bit as an impostor being that designing is not exactly one of the things on my daily duties at the office.

"You know your agency is one of the many I'm considering to replace my last one... maybe you could answer a few questions for me?" Of course! Mr. Halifax! The CEO for Synery Cruise Lines! Neil told me he might be here because he knew he let go his previous agency... Apparently many companies come to these advertising conferences when they need to check out new perspective agencies. He told me to try and set a meeting with him, something I deemed almost impossible, considering I have no contacts, or know anyone in the business yet. This is great!

"Anything you need to know, Mr. Halifax."

"Please call me George." He offers me the box of cigars.

Oh, why not? One should try everything once, right? "Thank you – George." I say as I grab a cigar out of the wooden box. George lights it up for me and I inhale deeply; I think I look pretty cool for a second until I start coughing uncontrollably, remembering that cigars are not like cigarettes, which I smoked for a while in my early twenties – to impress a guy, okay say no more. Santi hands me my drink and I start laughing embarrassed, feeling like such a dud. "It's been a while…" I say not meeting their gaze.

They all laugh and raise their glasses to make a toast. I hope this guy doesn't think I'm a complete moron and changes his mind about going with the agency. To my relief he asks me a bunch of questions, which I manage to answer pretty cohesively. I feel like an idiot once more when he asks for a business card; I make up some excuse as to why I don't have any, and scribble the number down on a napkin. Trying to brush my inadequacy aside, I remember how Neil told me that they don't make business cards for the Junior. I'd have to wait until I was promoted and have to carry cards of all the other people in the office to give out when necessary. Well, I really didn't want to hand out cards with someone else's name on them, I just hope no one at the office will go through my desk drawer and find the huge stack of cards Neil gave me stashed in there.

"Thank you." George says taking the napkin and shoving it in his pocket. "I will have Lily call your office some time next week. Now, how about we have some fun! I've been working like a dog and I need to make up for it." He orders another round of drinks and slams his whiskey down in one shot.

After meeting practically everyone at this party, we hit the bar once more. Three attractive women in their early forties are eying George as they chat at the end of the bar. Without thinking it twice he buys them a drink. Santi starts talking to one of them and the woman instantly starts flirting with him. Biel and I stand to the side watching his friend in action, the guy is such a gigolo! But it's fun to watch him as this woman completely melts over him. George offers all of us another drink, but feeling like I've had enough for the evening I decline on this one. Biel also refuses as he puts down his half finished glass on the bar.

"Great guy, but he thinks he's still 22." Biel says as we watch George heavily flirting with the two women.

"What's Santi's story?" I ask him as Santi and the third woman lean over each other as in a very intimate conversation.

"He's recuperating from a girl who broke his heart in Spain."

"Oh. How long ago has it been?"

"Two years."

"That long?"

"Well… he took it very hard. She was the first girl he loved, and he swears it will be the last."

"That's a little cowardly, isn't it?"

"Cowardly… Mmm… I've never heard it put like that before."

Our conversation is broken by a loud giggle. George is whispering to one woman while the other provocatively massages his shoulders and pecks. By the bar are about half a dozen shot glasses.

"I think I rather miss this show, Biel." In a way this whole display is a bit comical, although I feel a little embarrassed for them. They are obviously very drunk and are getting too carried away.

"One more round of tequila shots for all." George tells the bartender as he grabs one of the women by the waist and pulls her to his lap.

"Just the three of you?" The bartender asks looking towards Santi and the third woman as they walk out of the ballroom, their arms tight around each other.

"Looks that way!" He slurs and then looks to us.

"We'll see you tomorrow, George." Biel says shaking his head.

"Nice to meet you, Sara. I'll make that appointment and thank you for the information!" He smiles and takes his shot in one gulp.

"Nice guy, but he's completely out of control…" I tell Biel laughing as we walk out of the ballroom.

"Poor George. He doesn't drink a lot, but when he does he really does. He also loves women and when they pay him any attention he will not hesitate."

As we walk through the hotel lobby, I notice that many others are coupled up on couches or by one of the many bars around the hotel. It seems that this must go on a lot at these conventions. I guess for people who are open to it, this must be a free for all. Add to that all the booze, and you get about the equivalent of a college party.

"Are you tired? Or do you want to hang around a little bit?" Biel asks looking towards the French doors that lead outside.

"I'm okay, I can stay up for a while more." I say not knowing exactly what else there is to do, but being that I don't feel like sleeping yet, I'm sure we can find something. Right?

Thirteen

"I'm sorry to keep you." He says sheepishly. "The truth is that I don't want to go to my room yet... I'm sure the show is in full force up there." Knowing he means that Santi and the woman must be having some drunken, noisy sex, I smile awkwardly and then I can't help but to start laughing. He does the same and then we just crack up uncontrollably. We decide to go get some water and then we sit outside by the pool.

"So what's the story with you?" Biel asks unexpectedly once we are outside.

"What do you mean?"

"Your friend Courtney mentioned something about a guy you were dating or something..."

"Oh, him." I roll my eyes and before I know it I launch into a full explanation of the whole fiasco the other night. Somehow, it feels good to talk about it. Telling someone helps me to unload, and talking to Biel is somehow really easy.

A half hour later, we're still talking when I feel a drop of rain. Some seconds later a lightning bolt followed by a very loud thunder prompts us to run back inside and just as we walk in it starts to downpour.

"Well, I guess it's a good time to call it a night, don't you think?" I ask looking at the incessant rain outside. But then it hits me that I have to cross the gardens to get to my room. Shit. I really don't feel like getting wet right now.

"Common, let's go, what floor are you in? Do you need me to walk you?" He says.

"Uh, no, no... I'm okay." I smile. "Really."

He starts walking towards the elevator and that's when I stop him.

"Look, I'm in one of the buildings outside." It just feels much better to speak the truth.

"Well, why didn't you say something before?" He asks smiling, like it's no big deal to him. "Look, if you like you can wait for the rain to pass in our room."

Seeing the look on my face he quickly adds, "Hey, hey, common, I'm not Santi... I'm not up to anything, you can hang out in my room as long as you need. Or you can stay down here and wait for the rain to pass here. But, it could rain for hours, and

I rather you not go around outside by yourself so late at night. Call me old fashioned if you want, but that's how I feel."

"Alright… if you put it that way." I ease up and smile at him.

"Hey, I've got tomato bread." He says with a half smile. "Those o d'heuvres at the party didn't do much for me…"

The rain is still coming down two hours later. We're on the couch full of tomato bread and half asleep. It's been quiet since we walked in the room, thankfully, but now some loud moaning is coming through the sliding wooden door to Santi's bedroom. Biel grunts as he goes over and knocks on the door; the moaning suddenly stops and we hear some girly giggles.

"I think I'll just go…" I say a little embarrassed. "Do you have a plastic garbage bag or something?"

"Listen, you can stay here, no problem." He assures me. "I'll sleep on the couch and you can take my bed. The partition door is pretty solid, it will be quiet in there…"

I mull this over for a second and decide that I really don't feel like taking the ten minute walk to my room and getting soaked. Besides, this room is so much better than mine, I love seeing the rain from the windows, and I'm practically falling asleep. I make sure Biel really means it and that I'm not in the way, he assures me its fine and hands me a long t-shirt and some shorts to sleep in.

I'm extremely cozy being under the covers with the rain pounding outside. I find myself thinking about our outing today around the island, I really had a fun time. Biel and Santi are turning out to be great friends. As the storm passes I drift to sleep, only to be awakened again by a super loud thunder. I open my eyes and see the alarm clock on the night stand, it's actually three hours later and it sounds like another storm is coming.

I get up and move the sheer curtain a little to look outside. Shit! I see someone sitting on a lounge chair out there, and my heart does a little skip, who could it be and how did they get there? I look again and with relief realize that it's Santi. I open the sliding door and walk outside to make sure he's alright.

"What are you doing out here?" I say whispering.

He smiles weakly when he sees me. "Oh, I couldn't sleep… I came out to watch the lightning" He then looks at me in sudden surprise. "What are you doing here?"

I tell him how I ended up here because of the rain and that Biel insisted I stay.

"I was wondering why he was sleeping on the couch…"

Just then a huge bolt brightens the sky and ocean making it daylight for about three seconds.

"Wow, it's beautiful…" I say staring out to the water. "Looks like another storm is coming."

"I think so too… I was hoping I could spend the rest of the night out here." He sits back rubbing his forehead, then notices my questioning look. "I shouldn't have brought that woman up here. I just do these things and then I don't feel good about it, you know…"

He goes on about the girl in Spain who dumped him, the one Biel mentioned earlier. It really seems he got hurt bad. I try to convince him that he should consider a relationship again. Obviously what he's doing is not working for him. He needs to put this behind him and try again. We watch as another lightning streaks bright across the clouds and then drizzle starts to fall. To my surprise, he then asks about Courtney again. He changes the subject quickly, leaving me to wonder… He doesn't pursue it, so I guess he's just making conversation.

The drizzle is now intensifying and as we run inside it starts coming down pretty heavily. Santi thanks me for the talk and slowly makes his way to his room. We came in through the main sliding door, which goes to where Biel is sleeping on the couch, so I close the door carefully, trying not to wake him. He is sleeping so peacefully on the couch and I have to admit that he looks so… I don't know, sweet? Undoubtedly he is good looking… Argh! It's way too late! I shake the thought lose and get into the bed sighing.

The storm continues to rage outside and I fall asleep with images of the previous day rolling in my mind. It really was a great day.

A loud noise infiltrates my dreams until I open my eyes and see that it is daylight. I realize that the noise is the alarm clock going off on the night stand, it reads ten in the morning. I get up and open the partition door to find Biel cooking breakfast.

"Good morning!" He says smiling. He tells me that Santi is still sleeping and the woman who spent the night left earlier. "He wanted to go visit around the island again today, but he's pretty hung over... and between you and me I think a little cranky."

I tell him about our late night conversation and that maybe he should persuade him a little to try a relationship or something.

"Maybe that's a good idea." He winks and flips the eggs he has on the pan. "Listen, I'm going to try to find those waterfalls today, do you want to come?"

As I walk out of Biel and Santi's room I run into a couple of people who came out of a room a few of doors down. They both look at me as I close the door so I say hello. One of them mumbles a low hello and looks at the other one frowning. Weird. I guess they are having an argument or something. I blow it off and start walking towards the elevators and to my room so I can shower and change.

Biel picks me up about an hour later and we drive off in the jeep in search of the waterfalls. We finally find them, but not before we run into all sorts of beautiful beaches and cliffs. We also make a point to go to the beach I found yesterday and take a swim there. It looks more beautiful today than it did yesterday. It isn't until after three that we finally make it to the waterfalls and they are absolutely beautiful. For a second I wish I was there with Ivan, because the place is so damn romantic! But that thought suddenly disappears as I see Biel taking his shirt off and heading for the water. I notice for the gazillionth time how good looking he really is and have to stop myself from staring at him.

I take my cover-up off and also head towards the water, making sure my bathing suit is all in place. Biel starts splashing me with water as I get into the little lagoon under the waterfall. I splash him back and we go into an all out water war. I can't remember having this much fun in a long time. We spend about an hour swimming and splashing around until we realize it's getting late and should start heading back to the hotel.

Biel gets out first and then offers his hand to help me up, I grab it and suddenly find myself standing right in front of him still holding his hand. We stand there for a few seconds staring at each other when I feel a chill. I nervously giggle and step away feeling a little embarrassed.

"Race you to the jeep!" I say and start to run. He takes off after me and we both get to the jeep at the same time as he looks at me laughing.

"You're fun... I like hanging out with you, Sara." He lays his towel on the driver's seat and then sits on it. I do the same and smile at him, feeling like I should say something more; but not sure if I'm reading too much into something that I'm probably imagining, I leave it at that. The drive back is over way too soon. Heck, the day is over way too soon! Although I have to say that I'm looking forward to a fun evening with the guys again and hopefully Santi will behave, and not sell out again to some horny older lady. I keep thinking that he and Courtney could be good for each other and the way he keeps asking about her... who knows?

I'm blow drying my hair when the room phone rings. Thinking that it's Biel or Santi calling to tell me where to meet them for dinner I answer with a cheerful "Hey!" I almost drop the phone when I hear Neil's voice on the other end.

"Sara?" He asks in an unsure tone.

"Uh, hello Neil…" Why is he calling me here? "How are you?"

"Mmmm… Sara, I have some good and bad news." Great. "Amy's all caught up for a couple of days on her work and will be able to make it to the conference for the rest of the week. Of course that means you'll have to come back here right away. She has a lot of copy that she needs typed up for when she comes back and it has to be done by the end of the week." He also tells me that he tried booking me on the late night flight, but it was full, so I'm on the first flight out at five thirty tomorrow morning. That way I can go straight to the office from the airport.

"Wouldn't it make more sense to just let you stay the rest of the week?" Biel says while we're having dinner at one of the hotel's restaurants. "I mean they'll spend all the extra money for plane trips and all that. It's very strange, isn't it?"

"And they have Amy fly on first class, and she stays in one of those luxury rooms on the top floors." I say as I savor my delicious steak. "I don't know, I guess she has some people she must need to talk to or something." I think by now the guys must know that I'm on the lower end of my office's food chain. At first I wanted them to think that I was a regular designer, but now that I feel comfortable around them I don't care if they know that I'm just the Junior. Besides, they know you have to start somewhere and I'm sure they will remain my friends and see me climb up the ladder.

I decide to stay up until it's time to go to the airport. I don't see the point in waking up at three in the morning to be there with enough time for my five thirty flight. I already packed everything so all I have to do is grab my stuff and be off. Santi and Biel say they will stay up with me, we'll just hang out at the bars until it's time to go. Right after dinner we're due at the Ballroom for some speeches and then more mingling with the Convention people.

"How will you be getting to the airport?" Biel asks when we're at the ballroom bar getting a drink.

"I'll just have the front desk call a cab or something." He scoffs, and tells me that he'll drive me. "That's alright, Biel you don't have to, you'll need to go to bed sometime!"

"Hey, don't worry about it! I don't mind at all." He raises his drink to mine. "Cheers to a couple of very fun days!"

"Cheers!"

I meet a few more people that Biel and Santi know, who say they will consider Tivoli-Barnes for their advertising. Most sound sincere, but I think once everyone is back at work and the euphoria of the fun atmosphere is gone, they will forget half the things they talked about. I also end up telling Biel that I really didn't forget my business cards, but that the truth is I don't have any. Not with my name on them anyway. He laughs when I tell him about the stack I 'accidentally' left in my drawer back at the office.

A few hours later I'm saying good-bye to Biel at the terminal. Santi stayed at the hotel, he looked really tired and went to bed. I am glad to say he stuck to his word that he'd go to bed alone.

"Biel, thank you so much for everything." I tell him, finding myself not wanting to leave. "I had a great time thanks to you guys."

"I had fun too, I will see you soon when we come back this weekend." He kisses me on each cheek and then gives me a bear hug. I stand glued for a few seconds before I force myself to move towards the security check belt. "Have a safe trip. I will call you."

I stop and turn to him. "I never gave you my number…"

"I'll… see you at the beach, I know where you live!" He shrugs and smiles. I wave to him and go through the security check point.

I'm seated by the gate waiting to board when they call me to the information desk. The girl behind the counter looks at my ticket, types something on the computer and then marks my boarding pass with some kind of code. She then smiles and tells me to have a seat.

Too tired to inquire what that was about, I just go and sit. A few minutes later they start boarding. When I get into the plane the flight attendant looks at my boarding pass and pleasantly tells me to follow her. She leads me into first class and motions me to sit down. I'm quite puzzled by all this and quietly tell her that my ticket was for coach.

121

"You have been upgraded to first class, by courtesy of the pilot." She smiles and before I can ask why she says she'll be back to take my drink order in a few minutes. I'm left here bewildered to figure this one out. Hey, if the pilot wants me in First Class, who am I to argue? To my delight no one claims the seat next to mine, so I'm left with two huge seats all to myself. I try to sleep, but find myself thinking about the past two days over and over. Flashbacks of the beaches, the waterfalls, Biel and I in the waterfalls, the fun nights at the ballrooms and Biel and Santi's room, all keep flooding my mind. I wish I could've stayed longer.

Fourteen

Marcia is hanging the phone up as I walk in to the office. She looks me up and down and gasps dismayed.

"Today is a walk-around day!" She exclaims. "Why are you dressed like that?"

I want to tell her that besides the fact that I haven't slept yet, that I just come from the airport, and that the walk-arounds are always on Mondays, how the hell was I supposed to know about the damn walk-around? But just then Amy comes up to me exasperated and leads me to her office.

"I thought you were going to St. Croix?" I ask surprised to see her there.

"My flight isn't until three, Neil wanted me here for the walk-around. Surely, he told you that we were having one today when he called you at the hotel, didn't he?" She's glaring at me, but then looks at my luggage. "Good, you have your clothes. Go change, quick!"

I don't waste time arguing, but I really do not remember Neil saying anything about any walk-around today. I go to the bathroom to change because I want a fresh set of underwear so at least I can feel semi clean. I'm not about to get naked in my closet without a door. Amy sees me go the other way to the bathroom and I hear her calling me. I ignore her and make a run for it dragging my suitcase behind me.

Luckily I packed the suit I bought the other day, and it's clean since I didn't wear it once on the trip. Unfortunately, it's not that long since the last walk-around, I hope no one remembers I wore it then. Amy purses her lips when she sees the suit and Neil keeps looking at me in a funny way. Yup, they definitely recognize it. Of course, as I suspected, Mr. Tivoli's son – who's doing the walk around on his own - hardly notices me, let alone my suit.

Before Amy leaves for the airport she leaves me a long list of things to do along with about 50 pages of text to type into the computer. It's mostly text for the vegetable account, but there are also other accounts as well each separated by paper clips. I try typing some of the pages, but my eyes can hardly stay open. I go get some coffee to keep me awake but It really doesn't help, although the walk to the break room feels refreshing.

Looking out the window as I walk back to my office, I get a flashback of the beach I found with Biel and Santi. I suddenly have an urge to call Biel and quickly realize that I don't have his cell number. I guess I could call the room, but I doubt he's there; I'm sure he and Santi are touring the island swimming in the clear water of some beautiful beach. I try to clear my head as I sit at my desk and make my eyes stay open.

"Uh, Sara, I will be wanting to speak with you..." Neil's head appears from behind the doorway and I jump up at the sound of his voice. "I'm really busy today, but perhaps tomorrow or Monday. Keep this in mind and remind me if I forget."

I force a smile. "Sure." He then taps his fingers on the doorway, nods and disappears.

I wonder what that's about, I don't think I did anything wrong, did I? Maybe someone I met at the convention called and said I referred them, hey maybe this is a step towards my promotion! I spend the rest of the afternoon trying to type some of the text Amy left me, but I just can't seem to focus on the screen. My eyes are so heavy and tired that I could go to sleep right here on the desk.

After about ten coffees, five trips to the bathroom, three trips downstairs and back, it actually feels closer to going home. It's six o'clock and I anticipate everyone will start to go home soon. Delirious and almost unconscious, however, I'm dismayed when at seven o'clock everyone is still hard at work, eyes glued to their computer screens. I am practically out when at about seven thirty, Larry peeks his head into my office. I think I'm looking at him with crossed eyes, but I can't even tell at this point.

"Listen, I know you must be really tired from your trip and all," He says sympathetically. "Neil just left, why don't you go home ad I'll take care of shutting everything off."

I get up as fast as I can and grab my stuff, I thank Larry profusely and make my way out straight for home. Did I just give him a kiss on his cheek? No… Could I have? I mean it was my first impulse when he came to rescue me, but I'm so out of it I can't think straight. Oh well, what's done is done I guess…

I think of buying another coffee for the ride home, but decide against it because it would take too long. Instead I splash my face with some water from the drinking fountain in the lobby and head for the parking lot.

"Sara! Hi! I thought you weren't coming back until Friday…" Courtney says as she opens the door and helps me with my bags. I realize I forgot to call her to say I was back early. "Wow, are you okay, you look awful."

I want to tell her the whole story, but only manage a short version of it. "Neil called, had to come back early, got on pre-dawn flight, no sleep, work all day, walk-around, Amy a billion pages of typing, day took forever I need the bed… I will tell you more tomorrow… Lots to tell you, lots, lots, lots…" I start to walk towards my room but stop by the couch, it looks so soft and comfortable. I collapse on it and my eyes close. Ahhhhh heaven…

"You must be exhausted." Courtney says and walks away somewhere; I start to drift away as I feel a blanket being placed on me. I feel so cozy I could stay here forever.

An extremely annoying beep keeps sounding near my ear; I open my eyes to find the alarm clock screaming at me from the coffee table. I slap the snooze button and slowly sit up, my stomach growling loudly. I can't remember the last time I ate something, was it a granola bar from the vending machine at the office sometime yesterday afternoon...? The smell of food reaches me and for a second it's like... tomato bread! But then I realize it's more like a frying smell, I go to the kitchen and find Courtney cooking eggs and bacon.

"Good morning! I didn't think you were ever going to shut that noise off. Sleep well?"

"Yeah, thanks for setting the alarm." I tell her groggily, eying the strips of bacon on the counter. "Mind if I take one?" I reach for one and start to tell her about the trip. She seems mildly interested when I tell her about Santi's inquiries about her. I go on telling her about the trips we took around the island and the nights drinking at the ballroom bars. She looks at me in shock when I tell her about spending the night in their room.

"You mean, nothing happened? Nothing at all?" She's looking at me like I have four eyes. "After all that fun you had together and you didn't even have the slightest urge to at least kiss or anything?"

"No! We were just friends hanging out, there's nothing else there, I mean Biel's cute and everything, but... we're friends."

She tips her head sideways and stares at me ruefully. "Right..." She finishes cooking the eggs and puts them on our plates. "So… you said Santi was asking for me, but wasn't he in the other bedroom with some old lady or something?"

Oops, maybe I shouldn't have mentioned that…

When I get to work Neil calls me to his office before I can even put my things down. I walk in and he asks me to close the door behind me.

"Have a seat, please." He motions to the chair in front of his desk. I sit down feeling a little nervous. "Okay… mmmm, I've talked to someone who claims to have seen something that bothered me a little… I'm talking about someone who saw you while at St. Croix… Do you have anything to tell me about anything before I go on…?"

I look at him for a second, having no idea what he's talking about. "Um, no I don't think so."

"All right, well… it seems that a client of ours saw you… uh leaving someone's hotel room one morning. Is that correct?"

What? Is he kidding? "It was probably my friend's room."

"Oh?" He takes off his glasses and bites the earpiece.

"I ran into a couple of friends who were also at the convention."

"I see," Neil says putting his glasses back on. "The thing is, uhmmm… we try to promote a good image for ourselves and we don't want to give a wrong impression to our clients." He stops for a second and purses his lips into a quirky smile. "We expect you to be discreet when you are representing the agency. Surely you understand…?"

What is he insinuating exactly? "Uh, well, I understand that, but these were friends of mine that's all, I wasn't, uh, you know… it was raining outside and…"

"Yes, uhmmm, okay… Just make sure that you stay in your room, should something like this come up again." He smiles in that quirky way again and then adds, with a head jerk, "Clear?" This is awkward to say the least. I nod and quickly make my way out of his office.

Once back at my desk I can't help but feel bothered by Neil's insinuations. It's out of place for him to tell me to stay in my room, isn't it? Plus, how did this 'client' know what room I was in? Or whose room I came out of? It's just a little weird, to be honest.

I spend the morning typing the stuff for Amy and before I realize it, it's almost eleven. I take a break and go get a coffee downstairs in the cafeteria. I stand behind a man who is ordering as I wait my turn and when he turns and looks sideways, I realize that it's Mr. Tivoli, Sr., he sees me and smiles.

"How are you?" I say smiling back. It doesn't hurt to get on his good side, does it?

"You're the new girl in the Art Department, aren't you?" He says looking at me over his glasses. I nod. "How is it going for you over there?"

"Oh, it's going well, thank you." I say and smile again, hoping I sound convincing enough.

He sort of smirks and then pats me on the shoulder. "You seem nice, I think you'll be okay. Don't take things too seriously.

If you ever need to talk about anything I'm on the top floor. I suspect it won't be long before you will…" He smiles, then takes his decaf from the cashier and walks away. Mmmm, What does he mean by that? Why would I need to talk to him about anything? Oh well, the offer is nice and I'll keep it in mind; who knows maybe I'll need some advice on how to get a promotion or something.

Fifteen

Saturday is finally here and I sleep almost half of it away; but I really feel great when I wake up. Looking out the window towards the beach I get a jolt in my stomach as I realize that Biel and Santi should be back today. I put some coffee to brew and walk out to the balcony; the warm breeze feels great. Looking out towards the water I spot Courtney and Lydia under the umbrella, they are with a couple of the beach boys and sure enough, one of them is Santi. I pour the coffee into a tumbler, take a granola bar, grab my beach bag and make my way downstairs to the glorious beach.

"Hey, it's the Sleeping Beauty!" Biel says as he hugs me and gives me a kiss on each cheek. "We missed you after you left..."

"I know, I wished I could've stayed with you guys." I say as I look around for Biel. "So when did you guys get back?"

"Last night, well… I did, anyway. Biel had to get on another flight and go to Spain."

"What? Why?" I hear myself sounding a little frantic so I add trying to appear more relaxed. "Was that not enough time off for him?" I say laughing lightly.

"Well, his grandma got sick… and he's very close with her so he left right away." He says. "But, he called this morning that she'll be okay it's nothing serious and he'll probably be coming back soon."

"Oh." I say sheepishly. I can't help but get a sinking feeling, I hope I'll see him again; it was nice getting to know him, he really became a good friend in these few days, as has Santi.

The rest of the day flies by and we don't leave the beach until almost seven thirty. The first thing I find myself doing when we get back into the apartment is look at the answer machine.

"Sweetie, I don't think he's back from Spain yet!" Courtney laughs as she sees me glancing for the machine's blinking light.

"I – I'm not checking for that! I just don't want Neil calling me in to work tomorrow or something…" I sort of was thinking about a call from Biel, but that's because it would be nice to hear from him. But I don't want Courtney getting the wrong idea or anything. Besides come to think of it, I don't think he even has my number, does he?

Lydia and Rosie pick us up at around ten and we meet the beach boys at the cinema. We end up seeing some fun action movie that leaves us with a wanting for more adventure; so we all head downtown for a drink. We agree on the Deep Cellar, and once there we start with the first round that Santi insists on paying for. Courtney, sitting next to him, has a googley eye expression that I solemn see on her when it comes to a guy.

The rest of the night turns out to be quite fun. We spend half of it dancing with that slight buzz you get after a couple of drinks. I can see the chemistry growing between Santi and Courtney all through the evening, even though I know she is trying to restrain herself because of what I told her about Santi's little adventures in St. Croix. This, however, tells me that she is starting to care about him, otherwise as hot as this guy is she wouldn't miss the chance to be all over him.

When we get home it's almost three in the morning. Since we're still high with excitement, Courtney starts to cook some eggs with toast.

"What did Santi say when you were saying good night?" She asks me trying to sound absentminded.

Santi drove us home since Lydia and Rosie live closer to the other guys and offered them a ride. When I was saying good night to him he told me that Biel had asked for my phone number. He said he asked if it was okay to call me, that he really wanted to keep in touch and was looking forward to talking.

"Is that all?" Courtney asks as she's fumbling with the eggs, trying to flip them over.

I get some coffee and start the coffee machine. "Well, he also said that Biel and I would be good for each other, which really took me by surprise because you know… we were all established as good friends, that was all. Then there's the thing with the girl who dumped him-" I stop talking when I see Courtney's expression and I smile. "Was he supposed to ask me… anything in particular?" She looks over at me, smiling foolishly.

"I just wondered, you know…" She slaps the eggs onto two plates. "I don't know why, though, he's not interested in a relationship."

"Are you?"

"Well… when I started to like him I felt like maybe that's what would be good for me. I think the reason a relationship didn't interest me before is because the guys I went out with did not make me feel the way Santi does."

"Maybe he feels the same, you should talk to him."

"Maybe…" Courtney puts the toast on our plates and hands me mine. "What about you?"

I pour coffee for both of us and we sit to eat what look to be very beat up over easy eggs.

"What? Biel?" I say unaffected. "I guess I'll wait and see if he calls, before I even think of anything else."

"Should I move the answer machine next to the front door, so you can see it as soon as you walk in?" She teases.

"Shut up!" I laugh as I lift a large piece of broken egg onto my toast.

Monday morning arrives way too quickly, I'm not even sitting at my desk when Amy rushes in asking for the stuff I typed for her. She claims it's not in the main drive and questions if I typed it at all. I saved it in the drive on Friday, I'm sure of it. She stands over my shoulder as I go in the computer and look and sure enough, it isn't there. I go get my original file that I kept in my own computer, transfer that into the main drive and put it in her folder.

Not five minutes later she's back. "Are you sure that's all of it? I think I gave you more than that." I take the pages she gave me and show her one by one. "Mmmm, well there are some missing here. I was sure I gave you all of them." She goes back to her office and comes back with about ten more pages full of scribbled text.

"Okay, here's all of them. I'll need these by this afternoon, it's very important that I get them as quickly as possible. Okay?" She purses her lips into a half smile and abruptly walks out. I find it strange that she's here so early, I'm always the first one in. I guess she has to get this project done. So, again, I find myself typing away. Two hours in and I find myself staring at Neil's head as it pokes into the doorway.

"Um, we were all thinking of some coffee and pastries... Can you break away a few minutes?" He takes his glasses off and sticks the earpiece in his mouth. Before I can respond he's already talking. "Thanks, just put it on your Corp Card, and I'll credit it later."

Since he said to use the Corp Card, I only have to go downstairs to get the stuff. That should only take about ten minutes or so. When I start to make the turn towards the reception area, I hear my name called and turn to see Neil behind me holding a piece of paper.

"Ahh… the gang decided they want French pastries… and, of course, they don't have those downstairs." He says as he holds the piece of paper to me. "There's a great bakery a couple of blocks east, here's a list of what everyone wants. Um, feel free to get whatever you like for yourself, okay? Thanks." He turns and walks back toward his office. Great.

As I walk down the street, I realize that he didn't tell me the name of this place. I'm hoping that I'll see some kind of French bakery a few blocks on. It's after ten blocks that I almost turn around when I see a French-Italian bakery. I'm going in, if this isn't it I hope they have good stuff, because this is what they are getting.

To my luck they pretty much have everything on the list, or at least something close. Less fortunate, however, is the price. I end up charging over seventy dollars worth of pastries on my bank card, which surprisingly doesn't get rejected. Last time I checked there wasn't much left in my account, so it's a good thing I'll get reimbursed for this. It takes all my coordination to walk back to the office holding six coffees and a huge box filled with fragile little pastries.

"This isn't the way my Profiteroles usually look…" Amy says as she takes her goodies out of the box.

Neil takes his pastry out of the box and lays it on the conference table. "Mmm... yeah, this éclair is not the usual one I get from Armand's either." Taking a step back, he looks at it studiously.

"Armand's?" I ask weakly.

"Yes, the name of the bakery where you got these...?" Neil says, looking at me skeptically.

Larry walks into the conference room, takes his croissant from the box and starts eating it. "Mmm, so good..." He mumbles as he walks back out to his office.

"You did go to Armand's, right?" Amy asks frowning.

I don't know, I didn't look at the damn name. "I... I guess. I mean I went east a few blocks like Neil said."

"Well yes, east a block then it's one turn to the right before you see the store." Neil tells me matter of factly. "But, uh... whatever. Do you have the receipt?"

I hand him the foot long slip of paper and proceed to take my own coffee and pastry out of the box.

"Mmmmm, on the receipt here it says Paneris, French-Italian bakery..." He studies the receipt further and before I can sneak out of the room he mentions how high the price is. "That's quite expensive... we try not to go there too often. Mmmm I hope the others won't mind paying so much..."

"Ten dollars for my Petit-Furs?!" Marcia exclaims as she looks at the receipt that Neil is holding. I leave the room before any of the others can drop their jaws about how much their little pastries cost me. Honestly, I don't see what the big deal is, when the lunches they get consist of twenty-dollar ham sandwiches and such.

I get home with the biggest headache, my eyes feel rectangular after having stared at the computer screen while I typed half a manuscript. The whole bakery thing is bothering me and Courtney's face when I tell her the story tells me I'm right feeling uneasy about it.

"You have to demand they pay you for the full price, Sara." Courtney sounds serious. "Are you sure this job is, you know… worth it and everything?"

"Yeah, I mean sometimes it gets a little… ridiculous, but it's only until I get promoted." I say, trying to feel optimistic. "I'll be moving up before I know it, until then I have to do all these assistant things, like picking up lunch and getting coffees. I know it's shitty work but I have to start somewhere, don't I?"

I go to sleep with Courtney's words on my mind. Maybe she's right. It does seem like this fetching of food and coffee gets out of hand sometimes. And all the menial things I do all day, the endless typing… I haven't worked on any designs since I got hired. Maybe I should take Mr. Tivoli up on his offer and go see him, if I tell him that I'm serious about advancing in the company, he'll talk to Neil or something. I mean, I have to get promoted sometime, don't I?

Sixteen

Mr. Tivoli's office occupies half of the top floor. A large amount of space is dedicated to the two reception areas that I had to go through before being admitted to his office. I'm sitting on a large sofa that looks out to a huge window while he prepares a drink that he insisted I have.

"Here you go, dear, a cola with no ice." He hands me a beautiful crystal glass.

"Thank you, Mr. Tivoli."

"Now, what can I do for you?" He settles himself on the other end of the couch with his own crystal glass filled with chilled grape juice.

I smile blankly. For some reason I feel like I forgot why I was here. All the things I practiced in my head to tell him are dissolving and I'm afraid of sounding like I'm complaining about a job I can't handle. Mr. Tivoli just looks at me with an expectant smile.

"Well, you see…" I study the creases in the glass, looking for the smart thing to say. "I was wondering…"

Awkward silence here.

"Yes?" Mr. Tivoli is still smiling pleasantly.

I straighten up and take a sip of my drink. "Well, sir, I just want to know how long does it take for a Junior in the Art Department to do more…" I stop to think of a good word. "More on the job tasks, like design and photo retouching, things like that?"

"A Junior?" He asks frowning.

"Yes. I mean I feel like maybe Neil doesn't trust me to do more responsible things. That's part of the reason I came up here to talk to you; Neil is hard to… approach. Well, I feel like he is anyway." Oh boy I think I'm rambling now.

"Junior?" He stares blankly. Why does he keep repeating it?

"Junior, that's my position at the Art Department, sir?" Surely he's familiar with the job positions at his firm…

"Sorry, dear, but what is a Junior?"

When Friday finally arrives, I feel myself relax at the prospect of two whole days off. I told Amy that I was going out of town for the weekend so they won't call me in. The last thing I need is to spend a weekend with her or Neil, the thought is enough to make me nauseous. This week has been absolute hell. Neil was nothing short of rude and Amy had me at the computer typing a book's worth of text for brochures that are still on spec. I then had to deal with an irate client that was fuming about a spelling error on his proof. The error was in fact Amy's because she gave me the text to type from and it was actually in Italian. That didn't stop her from putting me on the phone when he called so I could explain what happened. All this was over a proof that can be corrected, his brochure hasn't even printed yet.

On the positive side, I only had time to go get lunch for everyone twice, because Amy demanded her text be typed by Friday morning so she had time to correct it before finalizing it. Then, I worked on a design for about ten minutes one afternoon, before Neil came in screaming that the glue machine was nearly empty.

Courtney and I spend Friday night home because we're both exhausted, so we use the time to relax and catch up on the latest happenings. When I tell her about my visit to see Mr. Tivoli she can't stop laughing because he didn't know what the Junior was.

"Why's that so funny?" I ask her a little offended.

"Well, for being the big cheese of the company, they guy has no clue what's going on!" Courtney pauses to think and then continues more seriously. "I mean, either he's a useless company president, or there's something more here that we're missing."

"Like what?" I ask her getting curious.

"Maybe, he lets his son run things, he doesn't want to be burdened or wants to retire. They may have changed the name of your position, or they just created it for you… who knows, but you should snoop around a little."

"I don't know… I mean, how am I going to do that?" I picture myself going through file cabinets and getting caught by Neil. Ugh! I shiver at that visual.

"Ask questions." Courtney says. "Unsuspecting questions are the best way to find out information."

"Yeah, maybe." I guess I can do that, and another visit to Mr. Tivoli could also be helpful.

"Oh, shit! I almost forgot," Courtney says all of a sudden. "Biel left a message with his number in Spain, he asked for you to call or that he'd try calling again."

My heart jumps. "He did?"

I try to stay up late so I can call Biel, but I'm so tired that I keep dozing off as I try to focus on the television. There's a six hour difference between here and Spain, so I figure I should call no earlier than four a.m. our time. I mean it is Spain, they stay up late and wake up late, specially on weekends.

A loud noise from the television jerks me awake, it takes me a few seconds to realize I'm on the couch and a few more to remember why. I check my watch to see that it is about a quarter after five in the morning, I get the phone and reach for the little stickie note where Courtney wrote down Biel's number. I get ready to dial, but suddenly I feel nervous; I take a few breaths and punch the numbers on the keypad.

"Si?" A woman's voice answers after a few rings.

"Uh…, yes, Biel?" I ask realizing the woman probably doesn't speak English, she must think I'm pretty rude to not say anything more than Biel's name. She says a few words, which I guess to be something like 'hold on a second', and I hear the phone being put down. After a few seconds I hear the phone being picked up again followed by Biel's voice.

"Hi, it's Sara, from Florida…, uh… how are you?" I say nervously.

A beat or two go by before I hear Biel's voice again. "Sara! Hello! How are you doing?" He tells me how glad he is that I called and I feel myself relax. Before I know it an hour goes by and we're still talking; I tell him about work and he tells me about his grandmother, that she's feeling much better. He also tells me that he's not sure when he'll be back because his company had him back to work in the Barcelona office to do a project.

"I have to finish the work here now, before I can come back." Biel explains.

"Santi will really miss you, won't he?" I say and then a few seconds later, before I can stop myself, I add, "and so will I…"

I feel like I've said too much when he doesn't answer right away, but then, putting a knot in my throat, he asks why don't I go to Spain to visit him.

"You have some vacation days, no?" Biel asks convinced. "You should come, it will be fun."

Actually, I don't think I get any vacation days until after six months of being hired and I've been there only about four now. Damn. I still tell him that I'll see how it goes anyway. You never know, I don't want to completely dismiss the opportunity. We hang up after talking for an hour and a half; he promises to call me soon and tells me to think about going over there.

I fall asleep with a gushy feeling all over and dream of being in Spain with Biel. In my dream we're having a great time as he shows me around and then it all comes crashing down when Neil shows up with the glue machine. He is followed by Amy, who brings me a huge stack of papers to type up for her. Biel tells them to leave me alone that I'm on vacation, then I grab Amy's papers and stuff them in the glue machine. I tell them both that to compensate for bothering me out of the office, they have to get lunch for Biel and I.

"Em... Sara, today we're eating at noon, because we have a meeting at a quarter after one." Neil drones on as he leans on the doorway to my office. "We'd like to try the new deli that opened one block south on the corner, I think it's called Mootsies. Oh and here's the list." He hands me a piece of paper with a long list of items. "Thanks!" He says in a singing tone as he pushes off the wall with his shoulder and walks away.

Maybe it's time I took Courtney's advice and ask Larry some questions. He seems like an okay guy, maybe he has some advice on how to advance quicker into a regular graphic designer position.

"Well, honestly, you're like the second 'junior' we've had..." Larry is hesitant when I quietly corner him in the hallway on my way to get the lunch. "So it's kind of a new thing..."

"So there aren't any set time limits on when I could be promoted?" I say in a low tone, trying to sound vaguely curious, so he doesn't feel my anxiety.

"Actually, the last Junior left after one month... uh, that is... she got fired."

Larry also tells me that this Junior person complained a lot about her duties and Amy got fed up, so she convinced Neil to sack her. Great. That's reassuring.

"Well, I mean I'm not complaining or anything." I snicker, perhaps too obviously exaggerated. "You know, I was just curious."

"Hey, don't worry, really. Personally, I wouldn't blame you if you felt your job was a little... menial."

Just as I'm about to ask him about my chances to advance Neil approaches us with a frown.

"Ahhh, it's almost noon..." He looks at his watch and then at me with a stern gaze. I smile curtly and walk towards the exit.

Trying hard to keep my focus after a ten-minute explanation of how Neil did a design for a potato chip bag, I find myself very aware as I notice something peculiar. Amy has a printout of a design that looks very familiar; a design that I've seen before, or something very similar to the one I made for the vegetable account a while back. Hers has some different elements, but it's close enough that it could be the same. But I don't see how she could've gotten it since I never showed it to anyone. Unless... my computer is not password protected, she could've gone in there when I wasn't around. Would she do that?

She presents the design as an idea for the vegetable account. Apparently, the clients are not one hundred percent decided on what Neil has presented so far, so we were supposed to bring in ideas to the meeting to get something really outstanding to incorporate into Neil's design. According to him, his design is a bit too advanced for the vegetable client and they are not yet ready for something so innovative; he figures that by using another artist's more 'regular' ideas it will work better for the client's taste.

Everyone puts their prints in the middle of the table, or at least everyone who knew to bring them.

"Sara, ahhh, you don't have anything?" Neil asks raising an eyebrew.

I clear my throat and purse my lips. "I wasn't aware that we were to bring in anything."

"I'm sure Amy told you about it…"

"No, actually she didn't." I look at her with a straight face and then look over at her print laying on the table.

"Oh, I thought I did, I'm sorry." She says, showing concern as she puts a hand on her design, pulling it towards her. "But it's on the bulletin board in the printer room, you should've seen it there…" Right, the bulletin board everyone knows about, but forgot to mention, I suppose.

Neil goes around the table and talks about everyone's submission. When he gets to Amy's, he picks up the printout and studies it closely while he chews on his glasses earpiece.

"Mmmm, this is very interesting, Amy," He nods his head at her. "I like it, it's got definite potential. This could very well integrate with my own design…" Amy looks pleased, but is avoiding my gaze and just keeps looking at Neil as he talks about the design some more.

The rest of the day drags on and I'm really relieved when I get home and walk through the front door. As Courtney said she would do, the answer machine is on the foyer right next to the entrance. The message light is blinking so I hit the play messages button. A warm feeling emerges as I hear Biel's voice come out of the speaker. He says he'll call me back later, not to call him because it's his turn to pay for the long distance this time.

A couple of hours later I find myself immersed in a conversation about how Paella is made. Biel assures me it's not too hard to make, but it takes practice; acknowledging the complete disaster I am in the kitchen, I tell him he'll have to cook the paella. As we keep talking the conversation turns towards work and my job. I start to tell him about my frustrations, hoping maybe he has some good advice for me.

"How do you have time to design anything with all this other stuff they have you doing?" Biel asks incredulously. Shit. I forgot I told him and Santi that I was a Graphic Designer, as in a real Graphic Designer and not this Junior crap... I start stammering some unintelligible answer and then stop myself. I decide to just let him know the truth and tell him the reason I propped myself up at the advertising convention was so they wouldn't think I'm a loser. Boy, but do I feel like one right now though... Biel is silent for a second and then he starts laughing.

"I wouldn't think that!" He says, still laughing. "We all have to start somewhere. I made sandwiches before I started what I'm doing now."

He then goes on to tell me he knows there are some agencies that hire entry level workers and have them do all the crappy work and sometimes they never even get into any design work. This happens because they often have a receptionist that answers phones and does office work, but like all other departments except sometimes the executive offices, they are not designated any personal assistants. Hiring a 'Junior', lets them have their gophers and no one suspects a thing; the aspiring and unsuspecting graphic designer, is just happy to have a job so they don't mind doing extra work.

I sigh deeply as Biel finishes telling me this. I don't know if I should feel more angry or stupid. I guess a little of both, well, a lot of both is more like it.

"I'm not saying this is your case…" Biel says noticing my long silence. "I was just saying, you know, look out for that."

"That's alright… I mean, it makes sense. It explains a lot, when I went to talk to Mr. Tivoli he wasn't even aware of a Junior position." I say thoughtfully. I also tell him about Amy's suspicious design which looks like one of mine and how she presented it to the meeting today as if it was hers.

"No way! You can't let her do that, Sara!" After a pause he continues, "Wait… I know this could be too much of a coincidence, but you said her name is Amy, and she's a graphic designer?"

"Yes, that's right..." I say, my curiosity rising.

"Santi and I met someone called Amy at the convention the day after you left, I can't remember her last name..." He says in a mischievous tone. "She was around forty, pinkish skin and with reddish brown hair-"

"Cut into a bob, she's medium height and wears long flowery dresses and skirts?"

"Ah-ha, it has to be! She never said where she worked...."

"Her last name is Ferguson."

"Right! That's it, that was her!" He starts laughing.

"What's so funny?"

"Well..." He laughs again. "When I tell you what she did, you'll find it quite amusing yourself... to say the least."

Seventeen

After what Biel told me about Amy I can't look at her the same way. When I see her I have to do everything possible not to crack up in her face. It has actually made things easier at work, for I certainly don't feel like her air of superiority affects me anymore. In fact, after the conversation with Biel the other night, I feel much more daring at work; even though I should be upset that I'm being taken advantage of, if any of this 'junior' business is true. Not to mention, her stealing my design.

I've decided to implement a game plan for myself; any chance I get I will do designs for current projects and keep them for my portfolio; and not in the computer's hard drive either, I will burn them into CD's and take them home. This way if this job isn't going anywhere I'll have something to show and some experience for my next interview, wherever that might be. Meanwhile, I will try to find out more about what this 'junior' position consists of.

"Sara, I'll need for you to go to get us some coffee," Neil is doing one of his door leaning requests. "We have an important client coming… we can't give him that tar tasting stuff from downstairs." I've been working on some brochures all morning, using the text from a bunch of papers Amy gave me to type for this new client that I'm supposed to get the coffee for. Of course they'll never see them, but they will look good as part of my portfolio. I make sure to close all the programs and not leave any evidence of my work open before I go fetch the coffee. I wouldn't put it past Neil, or Amy to come snooping around when I'm not here.

Once in the coffee shop I look at the list Neil gave me with the types of lattes he wants. Three regulars and three nonfat, one for him and another for the client, whom word has it is a bit overweight; so to appease him Neil thought a nonfat for him would be best. I'm not sure whom the third nonfat would be for.

"Five regular lattes," I say to the lady behind the counter when it's my turn. "Uh… and one nonfat, please." No reason to jeopardize my own fat intake.

When I get back to the office the new client is already there.

"Neil wants the coffees in the conference room. They're already there waiting." Marcia says, happy to boss me around; I wonder if she knows Ivan's lovely receptionist-girlfriend, they would make great friends. "And one of the lattes was for me, I ordered a nonfat." She adds smiling smugly. I smile back, pretending to look for one of the 'nonfat' lattes, I hand it over to her, and take a sip of my own as I walk off towards the conference room sneering.

As I struggle to get the door open while holding all the coffees, Larry comes to my rescue and opens the door. I thank him as I go in, making a beeline for the table. As I put the lattes down I smile at the client, not really looking at him as I struggle not to spill coffee everywhere and mutter a quick hello to him.

"Oh, uh, yeah… didn't Marcia tell you to leave the coffees outside?" Neil chuckles nervously. "Um, here, give these to Amy and Tim." He grabs two lattes and hands them to me. He seems in such a hurry for me to leave and he can't even call me by my name in front of this client; talk about arrogant…

"Ah-ha! It is you!" I hear the client say as I start to make my way towards the door. Not certain who he's talking to I reluctantly look at him. "Sara! I'm glad you could make it after all! Where you going?"

I find myself looking at someone very familiar, and he's smiling very widely at me. All of a sudden I remember Mr. Halifax from the advertising convention, the one that said he would call the agency to get his advertising done when he bought us a bunch of drinks.

"Hello, how are you doing?" I say to him, ignoring Neil's stares. "I didn't know you decided to call, it's been a while."

"I know, I know… I had to take care of some other business dealings, but I finally called the other day and asked for you to work on our campaign." He smiles and looks over at Neil. "Then when I got here they told me that you couldn't work on our account because you had so much work already. I'm so glad you managed to fit us in!"

Neil smiles nervously as he looks from Mr. Halifax to me. "Yes, ahhh, it's good isn't it? Uh, of course, we are perfectly able to handle your advertising without Sara, you know, if she's too busy to do the best job for you." He chuckles forcibly. He's almost pleading.

"Oh, not at all! I'd be honored to work on Mr. Halifax's campaign." I say enthusiastically. I love the look on Neil's face; clearly, he wasn't expecting this. Ha! Now I'll be able to use the design I started after all. The conference room door opens and Amy walks in with Tim, she stares at me suspiciously. Neil tells her about me working on the campaign and she looks horrified.

Neil is forcing a smile, he sees Mr. Halifax eyeing the coffees. "Uh, Sara… which are the nonfat lattes?"

"Oh, no nonfat for me, thanks, I want the real thing." Mr. Halifax says.

"These two here are nonfat," I say to Amy and Tim. They all take their coffees and I have to stop myself from giggling as Amy takes a long sip of her 'nonfat' latte.

When I get home I'm pretty tired but when Courtney asks if I want to go with her, Biel, Lydia and --, I figure an evening out could be what I need. We decide to go eat some Mexican food, and then to a cool new place that just opened that serves all kinds of Martinis and exotic drinks called 'The Blue Room'. Today is 'Ladies Night' and we get two for one on all drinks, so I'm thinking on a week night, that could be a bad thing.

Once at 'The Blue Room', we find a table and order our first round. We start talking and before we know it we are finishing our second. Glad that my stomach is full from dinner, I don't object to the third, although I decide this will be my last one.

"Hey Sara, Court says that you've been talking with Biel a lot on the phone." Santi asks me smiling.

"Really?" Lydia asks curious.

"Yes we have actually, he mentioned for me to go to Spain and visit him." I tell them.

Santi looks at me surprised. "He did, really?" He nods, almost amazed. "So… when will you go? Or are you – going I mean?"

"Well, I don't know… I'd like to, but I have to get some vacation time first."

Santi nods slowly, I didn't think he'd be this interested… or is it concerned?

A while later, as I'm talking to Lydia I notice a lady seated a couple of tables away staring at us very intently. My attention is interrupted when Santi, seated next to me, taps me on the shoulder. He says something and not being able to hear him, he leans over closer.

"Do you want your fourth drink?" He asks into my ear. Being that I don't feel the effects of the other drinks and the length of time between them, I change my mind and decide to get it. Santi asks what type of drink I want and not being able to decide I tell him to pick something. I turn my attention back to the woman who was looking at us and notice that she is now glaring over at me. I can almost see the smoke coming out her ears. I turn to the others pointing this out to them.

"Oh my God!" Lydia almost squeals. "Don't you know who that is?

I discreetly look at her and notice that she's very elegant, older than us, possibly in her forties, but quite beautiful still, in a botoxy kind of way... She looks like one of those rich Palm Beach women, with money and husbands to spare. Although, I really can't say I recognize her.

"That's Lillian Monfae, from 'Love that Binds', the best soap opera ever!

"Well, since most of us work during the day, we wouldn't know." I tell Lydia, who as a freelancer can watch TV all day at home if she wants.

"You don't have to watch the show to know who she is, I mean she's the icon of daytime television!"

"Sure, if you say so..." I'm not much for soap operas. When I was home unemployed I liked watching the SciFi Channel as I circled the Classifieds.

"Why does she keep staring at you though?" Carl asks me as Santi comes to the table with our drinks.

"Who's staring at who?" Santi asks absentmindedly as he puts a martini glass containing a deep purple liquid with three blueberries at the top.

Courtney points at the lady who's been staring at us and he does a double take.

"Shit!" He sits down. "It's her!"

"I know isn't it cool!" Lydia says excitedly as she starts to get up. "I'm going to go ask her for an autograph!"

"NO!" Yells Santi pulling her back down and covering his face with his hand.

I start to laugh. "What's wrong Santi? Are you star struck or something?"

"No, no... it's just that—" He starts to say as Carl interrupts him.

"Hey, I remember now! Isn't that-?

"Yes, that's her." Santi says not moving his hand from his face and shaking his head.

We all look at each other. "What's this about?" Courtney asks Santi.

"Santi here..." Carl says as he starts to laugh. "Well he dated Mrs. Monfae for a while."

"What? No way! You stud!" Lydia looks at him with new eyes.

"Mrs.?" Courtney asks him, grimmacing.

"Well, I didn't know it at the time... I didn't even know who she was, I just got here from Spain and went to a party with someone from the office. They introduced us and... you know, I mean she was so beautiful, a little older but I didn't mind...."

"Yeah, and he spent three days at her mansion while her husband was away on business!" Carl adds.

Courtney is just glaring silently at Santi. He hesitates and then sheepishly keeps on explaining. "Well... I found out about the husband, and didn't want to continue with her, but she kept calling me."

Apparently this Lillian was in love with Santi and wouldn't let up. It even made the gossip papers that she had a secret affair, and was madly in love with some 'kid from Spain'. The husband brushed it off, but it is rumored that he knows his wife likes to run around with younger guys. Although she usually has her way with them and then continues on to the next one, not getting serious. With Santi though, she was 'swept off her feet' and her husband was not pleased with that at all. He actually warned Santi to stay away, and hardly believed him when he said he wasn't interested and didn't know who she was when they met.

He finally told her that he was getting married and he couldn't see her anymore; he changed apartments and all his phone numbers and finally got away from her.

"She almost sounds a little psycho!" I tell him as I look over to her table, but she's no longer sitting there. Relieved to not being stared at anymore, I turn back to Santi. "Whew, good thing she's gone!"

"So, this is the little tramp you left me for?" We all look up to find Lillian Monfae standing right by our table.

"Lilly!" Santi smiles awkwardly.

She turns to glare at me. I guess under other circumstances I would be apprehensive, but I feel sort of brave and looking at my empty martini glass I can see why.

I grab Santi's hand and look at her harshly. "Yes, Santi is mine now, and you can't have him anymore. He loves me and I love him." I say in my best soap opera character imitation.

"Really? We'll see how long that will last, you commoner nobody!" She turns to Santi. "I'm getting divorced you know, and the mansion will be all mine. You haven't forgotten about my giant bathtub, have you? The champagne? My stately sized closet? Oh, the memories... We could be magic again, I know you want it all back, my darling." She caresses his chin and he grabs her hand slowly pulling it away, not meeting her gaze.

"Why would he settle for one old hag like you when he has two younger women like us?" Courtney comes to Santi's other side and wraps her arms around his shoulders. "And we're all moving to my own mansion in Europe. You see, I'm filthy rich myself and I have everything he needs. After all, two young and beautiful rich women are much better than an old maid like yourself." She smiles sweetly and actually kisses Santi, heavily, as she hugs him. Lydia just sits there with her mouth open in a permanent stare as Carl tries hard not to burst out laughing.

I get up from my chair and hug him from his other side, skipping the kiss, I look at her and also smile. "You can see our Santi is very happy and doesn't need you." By this time a small crowd has gathered around and I even notice a few camera flashes. No one dares to approach Lillian though, being that she seems to be angrier by the minute.

Santi, thoroughly enjoying himself, waves at her goodbye as he tells her how sorry he is that it won't work out. She stumps her foot and dashes away to the exit. Two bodyguards that apparently were a few feet away watching, take off after her, one of them with a smile on his face trying not to laugh. Once she's gone Courtney and I go back to our seats, while a few onlookers clap at our acting stint. I can't help but feel a little guilty and sorry for Lillian, though.

"Hey, were are you going my sweeties?" Santi jokes as he stretches his arms towards us.

"That was so bad that it was good!" Carl says laughing. "I can't believe she bought it!"

"She lives in soap opera world, where everyone acts like that, she thinks that's the way everyone is…' Courtney says, as she looks at Santi.

"Thanks, guys that was fun." Santi takes a last sip from his drink.

"Well, I guess now I'll never have her autograph…" Lydia says looking at us with an exaggerated frown.

"I think you should cross "Binding Love" from your soap opera list." I tell Lydia.

"So where's this European mansion?" Santi asks Courtney.

"In France." Courtney answers casually.

"You really have a mansion?" Lydia says raising her eyebrows.

"Well… it's more like a small villa, and it's not mine really. It belongs to Sara's parents."

So that's where she got that from. I never talk about my parents villa, because it's like their hideaway. They go every year to stay a few months and then come back to the states.

"Aren't your parents Republicans?" Lydia asks me as she fumbles with her lipstick case. "What are they doing in France?"

"They're very diplomatic." I say defensively. "Besides, they've been going there for years and have many friends whom they have fun with talking about everything else other than politics."

"Here's to diplomacy!" Courtney raises her almost empty glass. We stay a little longer, before realizing how late it's getting. I almost forgot I have to work tomorrow.

Eighteen

Something weird is going on here today. I keep getting weird stares from everyone, when I walked in Marcia just made this weird snicker and then Neil gave me a long studious look before saying good morning. Amy just huffed and walked the other direction when she saw me coming down the hall. I'm trying to remember if I did anything, like forget to turn the printers or the glue machine off. But nothing comes to mind, in fact, before I left yesterday, I had to check twice on everything because I was half asleep all day after having been out at the Blue Room the night before.

"He's here, look professional!" Amy hisses as she pokes her head into my office.

"Who's here?"

"Mr. Tivoli, Jr. that is." She's practically panting.

"It's not Walk-Around day today is it?" I ask her, not really sure if it is or not, since these Walk-Arounds seem to always spring out of nowhere.

"No, it's not, but he's here for whatever reason and by himself. So look appropriate."

Not five minutes later Mr. Tivoli Jr. is in my closet. This is really strange because he never comes in here, I don't even think he knows this closet office exists.

"Hello," Mr. Tivoli Jr. says as he sits down on the folding chair in front of my desk. "Sara, isn't it?"

"Hi Mr. Tivoli, yes, it's Sara." I smile vaguely as I notice Amy walking by the doorway pretending not to look in.

"Please, call me Brian." He smiles curling one side of his lip.

"What can I do for you, Brian?" I ask getting a little curious as to this visit.

"Oh, nothing, I just wanted to stop by and say hello, I don't think I've come in and properly introduced myself." He leans back on his chair and looks around. He would be quite good looking if it weren't for his smug overconfidence. He's one of those types that always gets what he wants and expects everyone to fall at his feet.

"I've been here for... a whole four months now." I smile, being perhaps a little too patronizing, but he just seems so cocky!

"Have you? Well it's hard to see you back here... in what seems to be... a closet?" He does one of his sideways smiles again.

I smile back at him leaning forward a little. "It is a closet, Brian."

"Yeah… anyway, listen I was-" He stops talking when Neil pokes his head into the doorway.

"Oh." Is all Neil can say as his surprised face looks from Brian to me. He clears his throat and smiles at Brian. "Uh, sorry to interrupt, Brian… but Sara, here's the lunch list, we'll be eating at twelve thirty give or take." He puts the list on my desk and then tells Brian that the figures he wanted to see are ready.

"We'll continue this later," Brian says with that curled smile of his.

"Sure." I don't know what he thinks we need to continue, but whatever. He gets up and he and Neil go towards Neil's office.

Luckily, today's lunch was requested from the cafeteria downstairs for some reason, so I didn't have to go too far. By the strange looks I've been getting all day, I decide to just eat in my office so I can be alone. Marcia gave me another weird resentful stare when I came back from getting the food.

The strangeness did not stop here, at around three in the afternoon I get an email from Brian. I have to read it like five times before it actually sinks in.

Hi Sara. The reason I came to see you this morning is because I wanted to ask you if your 'significant others' would be alright with me taking you to dinner. I'm sure it's okay, maybe we can even all meet later… We could have quite an evening all of us, don't you think? Well anyway, meet me at Lucky's on the Beach on Friday night. I'll be waiting… Brian.

?????

'Significant others'? What the hell is this guy on?

"I think you should go." Courtney is serious as she says this.

"Come again?" I ask her with a huge scowl and she starts laughing.

"Don't make that face!" She continues to laugh. "No, seriously, you should go. Think about it."

"What is there to think about, Court? The guy's an arrogant wacko!"

"Sara, what have you been saying these days?" She stops but not long enough for me to answer. "You want to know what the deal is with this 'Junior' business, right?"

"Oh, no, no, no." I tell her as I realize what she's getting at. "Na-ha, I can find out other ways than to share more than a minute of my free time with this creep."

"Oh, c'mon, it's perfect! A great opportunity to dig and find out what you want."

"He didn't even ask me if I wanted to go, he just flat out assumes that I'll be there. What's worse, he can't even offer to pick me up, he just expects me to meet him there."

"That's great, this way you'll have the upper hand. He'll think he has you were he wants you, but you'll know better." Courtney says as if she's strategizing a game or something. "So you can make him believe you like him, while you extract information all along."

I don't know about this. I mean, yes, it's a good idea, but the thought of hanging out with this guy makes me nervous. And not in a good way. Courtney says that it will only be for a short time and once I have the information I want then I can stop seeing him.

"What do you think he means about my 'significant others'?" I ask, remembering what he wrote in the email.

"You got me there, girl. That's pretty strange."

The first thing I do when I get to work is turn the computer on and go straight to my email. After much thinking, I decided that if Brian doesn't attempt to contact me again about the date, I won't pursue it; I mean, what's the point? If the guy loses interest, I'm not about to go begging or anything. To my surprise there are way more emails in my inbox than usual, but I feel a wave of relief when none of them are from Brian. Yey!

My phone startles me as it starts ringing, it's probably Amy or Neil wanting something like an early lunch pick up or ten lattes.

"Hey!" I shudder as I realize whose voice it is. "Listen, I can't make it to dinner on Friday. So, I'll pick you up Sunday at 8 pm instead, so don't plan anything for that evening. How's that? Great. See you then."

"Uh, wait!" I manage to say before he hangs up.

"Yeah, quick, I'm in a hurry."

"Um, let's meet at the restaurant instead... I, uh, won't be home so I'll just go straight to the restaurant." I really don't want him to know where I live.

"Ahh, yeah sure, alright. I'll see you there." Click.

"You won't believe it!" Courtney's voice is piercing my ear as she yells through the phone receiver. "You have to see this for yourself, go now and get this week's Sunny Times and check out page fifty-six. Go get it and call me back."

I manage to sneak out and go to the kiosk next to the cafeteria without anyone seeing me. Neil tends to frown at breaks outside the time frame, unless it is to go get coffee or food, of course. I walk in and go straight to the newspaper rack; I spot the last couple of copies of the Sunny Times and take one. Not able to wait until I get back upstairs, I turn to page fifty-six. I don't know how long I'm standing there staring at the picture, when I feel the clerk staring at me questioningly. I quickly grab the other paper and put my money on the counter not even waiting for the change.

I can't believe my luck when I step into the elevator. Standing there looking at me at me with a smirk and a wink is none other than Brian.

"Hey you..." He looks down at the papers I'm holding. "That's a great article and picture..." He says smirking and before I can answer he continues. "I must say, I didn't expect you to be... you know, into that. I have to say, I'm... liking it." He gives me the slimiest look and I shudder in disgust. I'm about to tell him off when the elevator door opens, and I find myself in front of Neil. He looks curiously from me to Brian as he pats him on the arm.

"How's it going?" Neil smiles at Brian and then turns to me. "Uh... I was wondering where you were Sara, I need you to do something if you would please."

"Don't worry, she's all yours, we were just having a chat, weren't we?" He smiles at me again in that oily way. "I'll see you Sunday, for dinner, alright? Neil, let's go in your office, buddy, I need to go over some things with you."

"Sure thing, Brian. Sara just go to Amy's office she'll tell you what you need to do, alright?"

Before I go to see Amy I take the newspapers to my office and put them in my drawer. I'll have to wait to read the whole thing, I'm anxious to see what it says. Although by the way Brian is behaving, I can imagine what it is.

"Please sit." Amy says as she goes around the desk and takes her own seat. "First of all, I just want to say that you shouldn't expect nothing to change just because Brian has expressed an interest in you. You still have to do the same work and shouldn't expect any special treatment or anything." She pauses to give me a piercing look. "Besides, as you may know, Brian is not exactly interested in serious relationships with nice girls, he's more into flings with girls like yourself. I gather he's noticed you for your recent display of character from that article in the gossip paper." She pauses and smirks slightly. "Anyway, we don't put too much emphasis on employees' personal lives and choices, as long as they do their work."

At this point I'm just completely speechless. I can't believe this snake of a woman is saying this shit. I'm just about to confront her with the secret I know about her, form the convention, when Neil walks in. I can feel my face burning as I try to calm myself down. He looks from Amy to me raising an eyebrow as if to let us know he's aware he walked into something interesting.

"Ahh, excuse me Amy, if I could ask you something..." I start to make my way out as I hear Neil ask Amy about her design for the Nu-Vegetable account. The very same one she took from me. It takes all I have for me not to turn around and punch her out; so I make a vow to myself to make it known somehow how exactly she got those designs.

When I return to my desk I find a folder on top of my keyboard. As I look through it I realize it's the file for Mr. Halifax; I guess I am to work on his campaign after all. It would be nice if Neil, or whomever left the folder here, would tell me a little bit of what I'm supposed to do. I suppose I could call Mr. Halifax myself and ask him directly, but that might not look too professional. I know they have a set way of working on designs for clients and I think leaving me pretty much in the dark with this is a deliberate move due to the circumstances in which I landed the campaign in the first place.

I look through the files to see if I can find anything that could help me figure out what he'd is looking for; to my surprise I see that he has left good instructions on what he wants. He needs a brochure, stationary and a new logo. As far as the design style goes he left notes saying that I have free reign. It looks pretty doable and feeling pretty creative at the moment I decide to start on it right away.

Just as I open a new document in Photoshop, I'm interrupted by a too familiar voice coming from the doorway. "Ahhh… Sara, we're feeling pretty sluggish around the office… If you could please go get us some strong lattes… here's the list. Thanks." He puts the list on my desk and turns away back towards his office.

Nineteen

I walk into the Lucky's on the Beach restaurant and tell the hostess I'm meeting someone. Since Brian is not here yet, she seats me on a table for two so I can wait for him there. I get a drink and ask for some bread. I'm starving and I need something to hold me over until we order. I look around and notice that the place is packed, it's full of young couples mostly and feel a little out of place sitting by myself.

I'm on my second basket of bread and about to order another drink when a tap on my shoulder makes me jump. I turn to see Santi standing there grinning.

"Hey! How you doing? You're not here alone, are you??" He asks looking at the empty space in front of me. Glancing towards the entrance I explain the situation to him in a low voice. He laughs as he remembers the other night with the soap star, Lillian and quickly agrees to go back to his date when I say that maybe it's better if Brian doesn't see him. I told Brian that Santi doesn't approve of his 'girlfriends' going out with other guys, he only approves of other girls joining the relationship. It will probably give him feelings of grandeur to know that I'm 'sneaking around' just to be with him; hopefully this will help me get information out of him. I'm sure he thinks some kinky stuff must be in store for the near future and I can't wait to tell him otherwise as soon as I get what I need from him.

After Santi goes back to his seat I realize I've been waiting for over a half hour. I think this over and make up my mind to forget the whole thing and leave. I'm just about to stand up when I hear my name. I look up and see Brian standing there with a big grin.

"Hello gorgeous... were you going somewhere?" He says as he sits down. "You weren't waiting for too long, were you?"

"Yeah, actually I almost left." I say nicely, but trying to get my point across.

"Oh really? Sit down then, I'm here now. Order yet?" He opens the menu that the waitress just put in front of him.

You guessed it, it's going to be a long one.

The weekend could not have gotten here quick enough. I'm on cloud nine as I lay under my umbrella on my huge fluffy towel. I could stay here until the end of time. It's the perfect beach day and all I want to do is enjoy it to the fullest.

"So, you didn't get anything out at all from that idiot?" Courtney is the greatest friend, but sometimes she can be absolutely irksome.

"Can we talk about this later?" I ask her irritated, then as I see her looking a bit hurt I feel kind of guilty. "I'm sorry, it's just that this whole thing with work is getting to me."

"Well, just go out with him a couple more times and you should be able to find out enough to let you make a decision on whether you should quit and find something better."

The thought of another date with Brian gives me shivers. "I wish there was a better way to do this than to go out with that nasty egomaniac."

Courtney laughs. "Hey, what does Biel say about all this? Have you told him yet about your new man?"

"No. I can't tell him... he'll think I'm a sleaze."

"Oh Sarah, please! Are you kidding? You really have it bad for this guy, don't you?" She studies me and I turn to look at the ocean.

"I do not. I just don't want the guy to get the wrong impression about me, he's a nice friend."

"Give it up!" She shakes her head. "Oh and by the way, he called earlier, but you were already out here, so I told him you'd call later."

I try to play it cool, but inside I already feel the familiar butterflies. It takes a big effort not to run up to the apartment right now to call him. I try to relax and just enjoy the beach; besides I don't want him to think that all I can think of is calling him. I'm not yet sure how he feels and I'm getting more of a feeling that he views our relationship as that of good friends. He really hasn't hinted at anything else... then again neither have I, much to Courtney's dismay. She tells me I should just let him know how I feel, which I keep telling her is just friendship, but she doesn't buy it. She really knows me way too well.

"Santi says that it looks like Biel may stay in Spain for a while longer." Courtney says as she lays back down on her towel. "Has he mentioned again for you to go there and visit him?"

"Not since that one time a while back..." And that makes realize something, "So, you've been talking to Santi a lot lately, haven't you?"

"A little..." She shrugs her shoulders, smiling. "He's nice, we've become good friends."

"Friends? Mmmm, and you get on my case about Santi."

"Yes, because you like him and he probably likes you too. Santi's not into relationships and you know me... I can't get serious with anyone. We're just good friends, we really get along well."

"Right." I smile. "We'll see..."

"Who was that I saw him with last night at Lucky's on the Beach?" I ask her curious to find out if she knows he was out on a date.

Just then, a male voice says hello and before I can turn to see who it is, Courtney sits up and smiles widely at a tall figure standing by our umbrella. I look up and see that it is Santi, I say hi back to him and he turns to Courtney with a big smile.

Monday morning greets me with a stack of papers left on my desk to be typed for Amy. That in itself is bad enough, but what makes it worse is what I just saw on the Due Board, which hangs out in the hallway with all the due dates for projects being worked on. It says that the preliminary designs for Mr. Halifax are due tomorrow morning. I rarely ever need to look at this board, but still, I could have sworn that Mr. Halifax's stuff wasn't due until later in the week. Of course, to make my Monday even merrier, I'm absolutely bummed out that Biel did not call me back after I left him a message on Saturday evening.

I decide to start on the typing and get that out of the way, so I can concentrate on the designs for the rest of the day. Halfway through the first page, I jump up when a voice on the doorway startles me.

"Good morning…" I look up to see a smiling Brian making his way in. "So, how are we today?" He sits down across from me and tilts his head sideways.

"Just great, thanks." I lie flatly. What does he want now? It's not like our date was the best success or anything.

"What are you doing next Thursday?" He picks up a paper clip from my desk. "I'd like to go to dinner again."

"Well—" I start to say as my phone rings. I stop to answer it.

"This is Sara."

"Sara! Hi, it's Biel, how are you?"

Shit. Unexpected, completely unexpected.

"Hello? Are you there?" Biel says when I don't respond.

"Yes! Yes, I'm sorry, I'm here."

"Ah… sorry to call you at your office…" He sounds apprehensive, "Is it a bad time?"

"No, no, of course not!" I look over at Brian, who is staring very curiously. I smile half heartedly.

"So, what time's good for you then?" Brian asks, ignoring the fact that I'm on the phone.

"Can you hold on for just a second?" I ask Biel and click the hold button. I hate that I'm being so rude, but I don't want him hearing me making plans to go to dinner with this guy.

"Who's that?" Brian points to the phone.

"Oh, a friend of mine." I try to sound dismissive. "Eight is good for me, for dinner that is."

"Ah… how about if we meet at eight thirty? I forgot I have something else planned before then."

"Sure, fine." I realize that Biel is calling long distance and putting him on hold is not really decent on my part. I reach for the hold button looking at Brian in hopes that he gets the message to leave.

"Hi, Biel, sorry for that, it's just kind of crazy here today." I say into the receiver in a low voice, looking up at Brian still sitting there listening.

"I'm sorry, I should have called you at home… I just wanted to talk and didn't think." He says sounding embarrassed.

"I was thinking Pietros, they have excellent food there." Brian says loudly and I smile acknowledging him.

"Don't worry, listen how about if I call you a little bit later?" I say to Biel feeling awful, he agrees and we hang up.

"You know, you should limit personal calls… Neil might say something." He tells me and then winks with a smug chuckle.

"Well, I have a lot of work and Neil will definitely say something if I don't get it done." I tell him with a laugh, hoping he'll get the hint. He sits still for a few seconds and finally gets up to leave.

"See you Thursday, unless I come by here before then… I'm kind of taking a liking to this little closet." And with that he's out the door. What a creep, I can't believe I agreed to go out with him again. I hope it's worth it.

I type as much as I can for the next hour and my mind goes back to the phone call with Biel. I feel terrible for having been so rude, but it was hard to talk to him with that idiot sitting there. I look around casually and see everyone is busy in their offices. I go get my printouts from the printer room and as I see no one waking around I go back to my office and quickly dial Biel's number. I'm glad it's him who answers and I dive into an apology about earlier. I tell him that the owner's son was in my office so I couldn't really talk, of course I skipped the part where he was asking me to go to dinner.

"Tivoli's son is there?" He asks surprised.

Surprised myself that he's so familiar with the people here I ask him more about it.

"Well, I heard that he might be helping his father out, but I never thought he'd actually be working or anything…" He says wryly."

"He's not only working, but pretty much in charge actually." When Biel doesn't say anything I continue. "His father's always here, he just doesn't seem to be very involved in the daily things at the office, it looks like he lets his son run things."

"Ha! That's funny…" He snickers.

"What do you mean? Do you know something?" I ask as I grow curious.

"Do you remember I said to you before how some companies hire junior level people and have them do the gopher type jobs?"

"Yes…"

"That's probably what he's doing, him and… what's his name… the Art Director, Ned or something…."

"Neil?"

"Yeah him, they're friends."

"How do you know so much about these people?"

"At the office over there in Florida everyone knows all these guys in the advertising agencies. They all know each other in the industry, so the gossip goes around…"

"So you think I'm just this gopher here?" I finch.

"I'm not sure… but it's possible." He pauses a second and continues. "Hey, I have an idea, since you know Brian why don't you go out somewhere and see if you can get him to talk? Go to dinner or something?"

That's interesting. "Mmmm, maybe…"

We talk for a while more as I keep typing and after we hang up I'm in a good mood, except for a nagging feeling about going out to dinner with Brian again, well maybe it's more the fact that Biel is suggesting I go to dinner with Brian. I don't know.

By the end of the day my fingers ache from all the typing. I had to go get coffee three times this afternoon because everyone was in a 'slump'. I also had to go get an emergency supply of printer paper because the paper supplier's truck broke down and he couldn't make his delivery today. Then I had to make a list for Marcia of other supplies that everyone needed so she could place the order in the morning. Why couldn't she make the list herself? Yeah, that would make sense wouldn't it?

Neil is the only one left in the office and I wish he'd leave already so I can turn everything off and get the hell out of here.

"Okay Sarah, I'm off." Finally. He's holding his hemp briefcase on one hand and leaning the other on the doorway as he looks at me with a small smile. "Ahh, so I trust you'll have the designs for Mr. Halifax first thing tomorrow then?"

What?? "Uh, tomorrow? I thought I had 'til Thursday... I wrote it down in my book and everything." I say as I start to get my calendar book out.

"Oh, no, no... we changed it, I'm sure Amy told you." He says raising his eyebrow and chewing on the end piece of his glasses. "You'll have it ready won't you? Or let me know if you can't and we'll take care of it."

"I'll have it, I'm actually almost done, so I'll have it, no problem." I lie.

"Alright…" He looks at me unconvinced. "See you in the morning. Oh, and make sure you have some coffee for us and Mr. Halifax when he comes in, he'll be here around eight… Good night." He turns and walks away.

Shit. Just great. What a bunch of 'you know whats'; no, let me just say it: what a bunch of Assholes! He and Amy are just determined to make me fail with Mr. Halifax, well I want to get things right for him even more now. So I have two options; One: I can stay here and work all damn night, or two: go home and try to do this on my ancient laptop. I just hope I didn't stash my little iBook too far into the closet; it may take hours, but I rather do that than stay here one more minute!

Twenty

"I might as well give up." I sigh heavily as Courtney comes into my room.

"I thought you were doing good, you've been at it for over two hours now." She looks at me with a pained expression.

"The computer keeps crashing, it doesn't have enough memory to handle these big files I'm working with." I say rebooting the computer for the 10th time. "I should know better, the poor thing is almost five years old, it worked well when I was in school, but now with the new programs it just can't do it. I doubt I'll even get one page of the brochure done."

Courtney's expression suddenly changes. "I have an idea. I'll be right back." She says excitedly.

"Where you going?" I say looking after her, but she's already out the door. I open the file again when the computer finishes rebooting. I spend another half hour working on it not managing to get very far. Running out of hope, I wonder where Courtney went with her grand idea; she's probably talking to Biel and forgot all about me. I'm just about to go to the kitchen and make some coffee when Courtney bursts in the room with Biel.

"I found your solution." She says all satisfied with herself.

"You did?" I ask puzzled.

"I think so!" He says as he slides his bag off his shoulder and onto the bed. He opens it and takes out a sleek Powerbook handing it over to me. "Try this, I have the latest software and this thing is very fast."

"Guys… I don't know what to say! Thanks so much! Biel, this is really nice of you I—"

"Don't worry, keep it as long as you need." He says, as Courtney looks at him affectionately. I knew she liked him more than she says. We make some coffee and then Biel helps me to get started by burning what I had so far on CD's so I can transfer it to his laptop. Once I'm all settled he and Courtney leave me alone to my task. It's almost midnight and although I have a competent computer to work with now, I'm still not even remotely close to having anything done.

I spend the next few hours on full force design mode, every so often I hear laughter coming from somewhere outside my room, so I assume Biel is still here. That's good, I'm glad for Courtney; I can hardly keep my eyes open as I put the finishing touches on the brochure. I figure I can still get a couple of hours sleep, so I set my alarm clock, turn the lights off and just drop on the bed.

I just about scare myself when I see my reflection on the elevator mirror. My eyes are red and puffy and my hair is a mess, I'm late as it is, but I have to make a run for the bathroom and try to fix myself before meeting with Mr. Halifax. I also don't want Neil to know that I was up all night working and give him and Amy the satisfaction that what they are trying to do is working.

As I was leaving the apartment, Courtney made sure I took some of her cucumber cream to put around the eyes. She swears it 'depuffs' them in minutes. I got a glance of Biel coming out of her room half asleep just as I was walking out the door and Courtney just giggled when I gave her a knowing look. I almost gave her the cream back because I think they will both need it if they are going to work... Although I'm glad I didn't because I can see it's already working and I need all I can get to look half way decent this morning.

"Where's the coffee?" I look up to see Amy staring at me with a screwed up face. I sigh as I continue taking my stuff out of my bag to get ready for the meeting.

"I'm sorry but I didn't have time to stop for it on my way in." I tell her.

"Please go get it right now before Mr. Halifax gets here." She spits out and abruptly turns away. I thought of not going and see what happens, but I really could use some coffee myself and it would be rude to only bring some for myself at the meeting and not for Mr. Halifax. So I decide to get some from the downstairs cafeteria instead of the preferred coffee place they always demand coffee from. Once there, I end up getting two lattes only, one with whole milk and one with skim.

"Hello Mr. Halifax! How are you?" I say to him walking into the meeting room and handing him his latte. The look on Neil's face is priceless when he realizes I didn't bring him one. Amy's look is not much different either when she walks in looking for her coffee; however, I think it's more than coffee she's coming around for.

As I proudly pull out a set of printouts and set them in front of Mr. Halifax, I can see Amy in the corner of my eye and she's ready to bark, Neil is chewing heavily on the end piece of his glasses. Although I'm showing lots of confidence on the outside, inside I'm petrified that Mr. Halifax won't like anything I've designed for him. As I finish laying all the pieces in front of him I try to read his face as he looks at them. He studies each of them carefully and very slowly as he hums and nods along. It seems like forever before he speaks and all three of us – Neil, Amy and I – are anticipating what he'll say. Of course, Amy and Neil are both hoping for the opposite of what I am.

"Mmmmm." Mr. Halifax starts. We all look at him, me trying not to seem too desperate. "Well, well, looks like you did quite a bit of work!" He smiles at me.

"Yes, I put a lot of thought into what would work for you." I tell him. "What do you think?"

"You know… I think I'll have a hard time with all these." He looks at the designs on the table again. I feel my heart drop.

"Oh. I'm sorry." I manage to say as I notice a flicker on Amy's eye.

"No, no! Don't be sorry! I just don't know which to pick! They're all quite wonderful!" He tells me as eh takes a gulp of his latte. "Could I take them and think it over for a few days?"

"Ahh… we usually don't let unfinished designs leave the building, specially without being catalogued as copyrighted, you know for ownership reasons…" Neil tells him.

"I've catalogued all of them already." I say quickly, feeling grateful that Larry showed me how to do it.

"Uh… alright then, in that case…" Neil says disappointed. "You can certainly take them, sorry about that."

"Great! Thank you. I'll need some time to go over them and make a decision. They're all fantastic! Thank you Sara."

"It's my pleasure, Mr. Halifax." I say hiding my overexcitement. "Let me know what you decide."

Walking back to my office, I'm full of glee and I can't take the smile off my face. I'm about to sit down at my computer as I notice a message memo propped up on my keyboard. There's a scribble on it that says to go see Mr. Tivoli right away. Wondering what this could be about, I grab my half empty coffee cup and head for the elevators, but I'm almost passed the reception desk when Neil calls after me.

"Sara, uh, we'll need to talk this afternoon when you get a chance… come by my office… say three o'clock? Alright?" He starts to turn and then looks at me again. "Where are you going? No one needs coffee, do they?"

"Mr. Tivoli asked to see her." Marcia says in a smug tone as she sneers at me.

"Oh, mmmm… okay then, see you at three." And he walks away.

I turn my back on Marcia, who is still sneering, and go towards the elevators. As I approach the 11th floor I start to get apprehensive; what if Mr. Tivoli knows about my dates with his son and thinks that I'm trying to get ahead by being with him and doing… yikes! I can't even bear to think about him like that, ugh! He's just so… ew!

I'm sitting on Mr. Tivoli's couch with my crystal glass full of coke as he sits across from me, a distant look on his face.

"Mr. Tivoli? Is there anything you wanted to talk about?" I hate to be so impatient, but I need to get back downstairs and start on the new stack of typing Amy tossed on my desk this morning; I don't want to stay too late tonight.

"Oh yes, yes… I'm sorry Sara." He puts his grape juice down and sits to face me. "I want to ask you some questions about your job."

I go on to describe my duties as best as possible, figuring I have nothing to lose I just spill it all out. The coffee, the lunches, typing etc… He also asks about Brian and although I hesitate, I tell him that he asked me on a couple of dates – as friends I say – and decide not to spill my plan for getting information about the

Junior job. I don't think it's a good idea to say this at this point, since I'm not sure what this whole thing is about.

"I see." He taps on his glass as he looks out the huge window, then looking back at me he stands up, takes my almost empty glass, and puts in on his desk along with his. "Well, thank you Sara. Your information has been very helpful. I need to do some things and then, if you don't mind I will talk to you some more in a few days."

"Sure... okay Mr. Tivoli." I smile uncertainly and start to walk towards the door.

"Have a good day, Sara." He smiles and sits at his desk, opening a notebook.

"You too, Mr. Tivoli." I walk out of his office more confused than when I went in.

"More wine?" Brian asks and without waiting for an answer he starts filling up my glass. We're only as far as the appetizers, but I'm already hoping to be done with this. Hopefully a third glass of wine will help me relax. I'm not looking to get plastered, though, that could prove badly. Although, I'm not too worried since Courtney and Biel have agreed to come a la 'incognito' and sit a few tables away, just in case.

"So Sarah, have you given anymore thought to my proposition?" He leans back on his chair. "We could have a lot of fun, me, you and your friend... I have a huge house all to myself."

"Yeah... about that." I say, suddenly feeling brave. "Listen, my friend and... um – our boyfriend, well they have actually decided to be together. Just the two of them. So, this thing with the three of us is not gonna happen."

"Really...?" He leans over frowning. "Well, listen I know quite a few girls, and they would be more than happy to—"

"No. The thing is that I'm not into that." I really feel brave now. "I don't want to take you on your proposition and that's final. What I do want is to ask you a few questions."

He just stares at me with amusement as he fills his glass with wine and empties the bottle. Taking advantage of my current courage I continue before I lose my confidence.

"What exactly is a Junior position? Why do I get the feeling that I'm being taken for a ride here? Can I even count on ever being promoted?" I stop to take a breath and a sip of wine.

"Listen... anything can be arranged, I can get you a promotion..." He smiles wryly. "Look, it doesn't even have to be you and your friend, by the looks of it, you'll be more than a handful all on your own!" He laughs as he shoves some calamari into his mouth.

I sigh heavily and stare at him as I prop my elbows on the table. "Look, Brian, the answer is NO. It will never happen. Got that?" At this point he will probably fire me himself, and spread who knows what rumors around he office, but right now I don't care. So I just go for it. "All I want to know is if I am wasting my time with this Junior job. Is there a chance for advancement, or is this just a gopher job you set up for your friend Neil?"

Brian, suddenly serious, stares at me for a few seconds. His whole demeanor changes and his expression appears almost vulnerable. "Well." He lets out a long sigh. "You're certainly not stupid. I had you figured all wrong…" He sits up straight and looks at me in a way that he almost resembles his father.

"I set it up for Neil to have someone that can do all the crappy work. The Junior. I sent the new position to HR with a description of a Junior Graphic Designer, knowing that anyone just starting out would take the job. This way Neil could have a helper, which he's not supposed to have, you know someone to do the things he's too lazy to do himself and the other designers won't do. Even the receptionist doesn't do any gopher work, which she actually should but…" he laughs knowingly, "that's sort of my fault there. She's quite good at some - things, so, uh, in exchange for those things… you know… anyway, that's why I promised Neil someone to do some of the menial work for the department."

"Wow, you're just the picture for moral standards, aren't you?" I say almost laughing.

"Listen, I know my father has spoken to you on some occasions…" He looks almost juvenile at the mention of his dad. "Please don't tell him this… I really hope to run the company some day and he just wouldn't stand for that."

"Can you blame him?" I say amazed. Then again, I think of Amy and what I found out about her and I don't doubt they're not the only ones acting so unethically. It probably goes on all over the building, just another day at the office.

Oh well, you know what? I don't really care. I just want to do my job, well, my real graphic designer job and mind my own business. As long as it doesn't interfere with me, I don't care what others do. Of course at this time this is interfering with my job, being that it was created due to Brian's inability to refuse any 'offerings' that may come his way in exchange for work incentives. But that will change. Either here or with another company, if that's what I have to do.

Twenty-one

After last night's dinner, I've done a lot of thinking. I decided to stay at Tivoli & Barnes for the time being so I can finish Mr. Halifax's account. Brian has agreed to step in if Neil or Amy threaten to fire me if I refuse to go get coffee or lunch, or anything, if I don't have time or just don't want to go. In return, I have agreed not to say anything about his arrangement with Neil on the Junior position to anyone, specially his dad – for now. We'll just play it cool, like nothing has happened, business as usual.

I still think of Brian as sleazy, but I have to give him credit for finally coming clean with me. I may have a chance now to get somewhere with my career and at least I know the truth. Once things were out on the open, I told him the truth myself – about Courtney, Santi and the whole thing with the soap opera star.

I hoped this would put an end to his advances, but he still found it in him to ask me out one more time. I had to laugh as I turned him down, even though he assured me that he was interested in a different way now. He said that I really had an impression on him and he realized he wanted to become a better person. Somehow, I think it will take a lot more for him to grow up; at least he's on his way. Although, judging by how he gazed at a cute girl on our way out of the restaurant last night and slipping a piece of paper in her back pocket after squeezing her behind while her friend looked on and giggled seductively at him, I don't think he'll be giving in to his old ways anytime soon.

My thoughts are interrupted by Neil's annoying voice as he walks into my closet and sits in front of me. Well, this is a first, he never comes in here, he always stands by the doorway or has me go to his office to talk. I look up at him expectantly and he just stares at me for a few seconds.

"Ahh, yes… I know I told you to come into my office yesterday at three to talk about some things, but I was really busy and couldn't do it then." He says as he takes off his glasses. Oops, I actually forgot all about the three o'clock talk, but since he thinks I didn't… we'll just go along with it. "So, as soon as Amy gets here we'll begin."

We sit there in silence for what seems like a century. He just stares at me while chewing his glasses and I do what I can to appear busy on my computer. I keep typing the same sentence over and over because it's hard to concentrate while the weirdo keeps staring at me. Just as I'm about to excuse myself to go to the bathroom, Amy walks in and I'm actually glad to see her for a change, of course this feeling doesn't last long. Seeing that there isn't another chair (mainly for lack of space) she sits on the edge of my desk as she spills an oily smile at me. She then turns to Neil changing her smile to a professional and serious nod.

"Sorry I'm late, Neil."

Seeing that this isn't going to be about a coffee run or anything like that, I start to wonder if Brian is a complete sleaze ball backstabber after all.

"Sara, when you were hired... I'm sure that the HR department told you what this job entails-" Amy starts to say but as she continues Neil cuts her off.

"We believe that you have already earned some, ah... time off, since you've been here a few months now." He looks at Amy before continuing as if to wait for her reaction, but keeps going without giving her a chance to respond. "So we feel this is a good time for you to take advantage of that time."

I look at him and wait for clarification on exactly what he means, but he just looks at me as if waiting for my reaction.

"Well... I, uh, how do you want me to take advantage of this, um, time? I'm not quite sure what you mean, Neil." As I ask this I see Amy rolling her eyes and shaking her head.

"You know, uh, vacation time?" She says sarcastically.

"We'd like you to go ahead and take your vacation at this time." Neil says as he gazes at me over his glasses while chewing on the earpiece..

What? A vacation, now?

"This way you'll be refreshed and ready to work when you come back." Amy smiles at me robotically.

"Well, I guess... I just didn't know that vacations were set to be taken at a certain time, I didn't have anything planned..." I smile weakly at them.

"They're not usually, not exactly, but with new employees we sometimes have to do it this way, plus with the way things go around here..." Amy starts to say.

"Things are really busy, we have to organize ourselves a little, then when you come back we'll be able to assign duties in a tidier fashion." Neil says with a wide fake smile.

"Mmm, okay." This sounds like a lot of hogwash to me, but whatever. I'm not too worried. "What about Mr. Halifax? He said he'd be calling soon with a decision on the designs."

"Oh, well... don't worry about that, we'll figure something out." Neil smiles smugly. "We can work on it for you while you're away, you've already made the designs so all we'd have to do is implement the one he chooses."

"We'll get the files from your computer." Amy says matter-of-factly, as if she'd never done that before...

"Right, okay." I don't think so. I have my own plans for Mr. Halifax's designs and they don't include Amy's paws all over them.

"You should go to Spain!" Courtney exclaims.

"What? Spain? Why would I go to Spain?"

"Why do you think, stupid? Biel!"

"Right, because surely, he's expecting me." I tell her rolling my eyes. "Look, I can't go anywhere, I have to be here so I can be in contact with Mr. Halifax." I emailed him right away to let him know I wouldn't be in the office but that I'd be working on his account anyway. He answered saying not to worry that he would be contacting me directly. He said he wants to make sure no one else works on his stuff.

"What if that twirp you work with goes into your computer and steals your files again?" Courtney asks.

"I already took care of that, I erased them from the hard drive and made a few copies on CD's." I tell her assured. "Which brings me to my next problem… I could go to the library and use the computer over there, or use my ancient iBook, or…"

Courtney looks at me and nods. "Or you could use Santi's computer." She sneers jokingly.

I shrug and give her my most hopeless look.

"Of course, I'm sure Santi won't mind if you use his laptop." She smiles. "He's coming over later, I'll tell him to bring it with him."

Courtney has finally admitted that she and Santi are pretty much together as a couple, but she's still playing it cool and wants to make sure that things will work out before saying she's committed. But I know her and I can say she's very taken by

Santi, just by seeing the way she acts with him, she's practically in the clouds.

When Santi comes over we all eat dinner together and as I expected Courtney brings up my vacation again.

"You should go see Biel." Santi says. "He asks about you all the time he'd be glad to see you and show you around."

"it sounds great, but I can't." I sigh and tell him about work, the dilemma with Mr. Halifax's designs and the whole deal.

"So you're basically not going because you don't have a computer to take with you?" Santi asks me.

"Yeah, but even if I did, isn't the electricity there different?" I say impressed at my own knowledge.

"So? Most computers come with dual electrical plugs now." Courtney says looking at me smiling.

"Take mine." Santi says, folding his arms.

"What, your computer?" Is he serious?

"Yes, take it, I can use the one I have in my office for a few days." He assures me. "You should go, Biel would be happy to see you."

Wow. I don't know what to say. Can I really be going to Spain? This is so sudden, but the more I think about it the more excited I get. I mean, why not? This could be a lot of fun and I always wanted to go to Europe, my parents always rave about it and I just never had the chance to go.

"I saw a lot of specials in the paper for European flights." Courtney says picking up a newspaper laying on the table. "you should look through it."

I take a deep breath. "Okay then, I guess you guys convinced me, I'm going to Spain!" I look at both of them and add. "And I'll just leave the apartment all to yourselves…"

"Oh, shut up!" Courtney says as her face reddens. "Here take the paper and start looking." She hands me the paper as Santi puts an arm around her kissing her forehead. As gooey and mushy as these two are (yes, I know, ugh!) I'm glad they are giving it a try, they're actually good together.

"So have you thought were you're going to stay?" Lydia asks turning on her beach towel to face me. Courtney spilled the news to her when she got to the apartment for an afternoon at the beach. I still can't believe it myself that I'm going, so I really haven't even come close to thinking where I'll be staying.

"I don't know… I guess I should figure it out, eh?" I answer.

"Well, what about Biel?" Lydia asks me. "Couldn't you stay with him?"

"No, I don't think so…" I quickly answer, although I can't help but get a jittery feeling at the prospect. "I might ask him if he can find me a decent hotel room or a bed and breakfast though."

"Argh, you're so boring! I'd be knocking on the guy's door the minute I got there!"

"I'm sure his mother would love the surprise visit."

"Oh, right… he's staying at his mother's…" She says disappointed. "Oh well, just make sure whatever hotel you stay at is near enough so you can hang out with the guy at least."

I sigh deeply. "I don't know… I'm still not sure if I should be doing this…"

"Oh shut up already, you're going and that's that."

I lay down on my towel to enjoy the last rays of the day. Afternoons are great on the beach, it's nearly empty and not as hot so it's perfect for relaxing.

I must have dozed off because the next thing I hear is Courtney calling my name as she shakes me awake. Santi is with her and he has a goofy smile on his face. They're both soaking wet, so I assume they must have been swimming and making out or whatever; couldn't they have taken another half hour or so? I'm so comfortable here…

"Are you sleeping out here tonight or what?" Courtney says as I notice that the sun's down and it's getting dark, I look next to me and see that Lydia isn't there anymore.

"Where's Lydia?" I ask looking around.

"Honey, she left over an hour ago, she even said bye to you!"

"Oh." I sit up rubbing my eyes. I really must've dozed off good.

"It's a good thing you're going on vacation, sweetie, you definitely need it." She says shaking her head at me. "Listen, Santi talked to Biel and he has a hotel room booked for you!"

"What? Already?" I ask her noticing how groggy I sound. "Uh, where? And…"

"Don't worry, it's perfect, it's a little hotel in the town where Biel's parents live, right near the beach." Santi says as he and Courtney start to pack their stuff.

I gather up my own beach stuff as well, all the while hoping that I can afford this place. It sounds great, but I'm still feeling uneasy about this whole trip.

"I think you're going to have a blast, I'm so jealous…" Courtney says longingly.

"Well" Santi looks at her smiling. "I'll be going there in a few months… and I'm expecting you to visit me."

"Ha! I'm so there! Just tell me when!" She kisses him on the cheek smiling from ear to ear. They are so sweet and cute together that it's almost sickening. And, no, I'm not jealous!

"So, have you been able to find out anything else about what's going on at your office?" Santi asks as we're walking back to the apartment.

"Not really, just that this vacation is a set up." I look at him matter-of-factly. "They want to get rid of me so that they can take over Mr. Halifax's account. They can't fire me right now because Mr. Tivoli is starting to suspect something, so they're pretty much forcing this vacation on me."

"I actually talked to Mr. Halifax a few days ago and he's insisting you do his work, just like he told you." Santi says.

"Yeah, he knows I'll be working on his things outside of the office." I explain. "But, he doesn't know yet that I'll be going to Spain… I hope he won't mind, I'm kind of worried that he may not go for that."

"Oh, I think he will…" Santi says confidently. "He really likes you."

I give him a strange look and he laughs.

"No, not like that… He likes your way, you know, your attitude and your work." He tells me. "I don't think he'd mind to wait until you come back from Spain to work on his things too."

"Well… I don't know, I rather not tell him I'm going to be out of the country." I say as we go up the steps to the front door of the apartment. "I don't want to give any reason for Amy to step her butt in and try to pawn her stuff on Mr. Halifax."

He looks at me sideways and smirks. "You don't trust this Amy at all, eh?"

"No. Not one bit." I say, although I have to laugh a little at my own paranoia.

"So you know Mr. Halifax pretty well, then?" Courtney asks Santi as she opens the door.

"Yes, Biel and I met him when he was getting new printers for his offices." He says as he holds the door open for us. "We told him that the best printer doesn't have to be the most expensive one, he was appreciative that we were honest with him."

"I'm just glad the guy trusts me enough to do all his design work." I say as I put my beach bag down and head for the refrigerator. "I hope I'll do a good job for him after all this, or it could prove very embarrassing…"

"Oh, you'll do fine." Courtney waves a hand at me as she takes the bottle of water I'm handing her. "When's your flight by the way?"

"In three days actually." As I say this I suddenly get a huge butterfly in my stomach, I'm really going!

"If you have a map, I'll show you where you'll be and how to get around a little bit."

The three of us spend the evening going over different roads in Spain and the best way to get to the Costa Brava — where Biel is staying — from the Barcelona airport. He insists I have Biel pick me up, but I tell him I don't want to bother him any more than I have to.

Twenty-two

I stretch my legs under the seat in front of me and try to relax. It's been three hours since we took off from Miami Airport and only in the first hour my butt was feeling like a piece of lead in the airplane seat. I was getting very anxious when I realized that I still had about seven and a half more hours until we were to land in Madrid. I got up and walked around a bit to get the circulation going again; I saw people reading books and magazines, or on their computers and I realized that the best way to make it through the flight was to relax and make the best of it.

I went to the bathroom and then went once more around the isles. When I got back in my seat I got my magazines out of my bag and loosened up a little as I started reading. Now I'm quite cozy in my cubic space, propped up with a couple of pillows and a fluffy blanket over my legs. Once you get over the small space and the fact that there are hundreds of other people within inches, it really is okay.

Just as I start to read an interesting article about how to tell when a guy likes you the flight attendants come around with the food trays. Well, come to think of it I'm quite hungry, so I grab my tray and seeing that the food doesn't look too bad I start to feel more positive about this long flight.

They play two movies after dinner, of which I watch both and afterwards they turn all the lights off so I sleep for a little while. When I wake up the pilot is making an announcement that breakfast will be coming around in the next few minutes and we'll be landing in Madrid in about an hour.

All my thoughts about this flying long distances being a piece of cake are fading away as I frantically walk around the Madrid terminal looking for the gate of my flight to Barcelona. When I asked someone on the information desk she said something about a bus. I don't think she understood me right so I figure I'll just find it on my own eventually. Seeing that it's five minutes passed the boarding time I panic and go to another information desk and this time I'll make them take me to the gate themselves if I have to.

As I approach the desk, I notice it's the same lady that helped me before, yep, her name tag reads 'Lucia' just like the other one; how did she get to this desk? It must be far from the other one, I've been walking around for like an hour! Well, whatever, I'm desperate and I need to get to this gate so I have to ask her again, if she thinks I'm an idiot that's the least of my worries.

"Yes, you have to go to the busses, which take you to the departure gates; it's too far away to go by foot. The bus leaves from the first floor downstairs." She says slowly but without a hint of sarcasm which makes me feel better. As she describes how to get to this bus stop I realize that this isn't a different information desk, but the very same one from before. I've been walking around in circles... boy, do I feel like a dolt now.

I guess I must have a blank look on my face, because the next thing Lucia calls a guard over and has him escort me to the bus stop. If I wasn't so relieved to be finally going to the right place, I'd feel like a total loser right now.

I get off on Terminal C, which is what Lucia and the guard said to do, and follow the yellow line to the gates. There I see the gate numbers and go towards the direction of gate 27C. I start to run frantically when I see that it's been fifteen minutes since the boarding time. As I approach the gate there's no one on the passenger area, although I can see the plane through the window. I'm glad to see that there are a couple of flight attendants behind the counter so I run up to them and slam my boarding pass on the desk. I can hardly speak because I'm so out of breath, but one of the ladies starts to talk first.

"Ms. Livingston?" She asks looking down at a piece of paper on the desk.

"Yes! I'm on this flight to Barcelona! Am I too late?" I gasp.

"We've been calling you on the airport intercom, the pilot was about to close the doors."

She takes my boarding pass and motions for me to follow her.

The intercom? I didn't hear a thing. "I couldn't find the gate and I was walking around all over the place and... well, uh, thanks for waiting." I say as we walk down the corridor to the plane's doors. She smiles and points me towards my seat as she gives me back my boarding pass. I hear her say something to another flight attendant in Spanish so I turn to walk down the isle. As I walk towards my row, being careful not to hit anyone, I notice the seated passengers glaring at me as I go by. I'm thankful when I reach my seat, all the way at the end, but feel even more like a moron when I hit the man next to me on the head with my heavy bag. "I'm so sorry, please forgive me, I'm really sorry." I say sheepishly as he waves his hand without looking at me and gives me a quiet 'm-hm' as he turns back to his book.

I take my magazine out of the bag and bury myself in it so I don't have to face anyone. I open to the page I left off and spend most of the hour long flight reading about how to tell if a guy likes you, my horoscope, good recipes for summer and the best exercise plan to lose ten pounds.

After I get my luggage from the conveyor belt thing, I spend forty five minutes waiting in line at customs. It's then I realize that I'm deathly tired. When I'm finally making my way towards the airport's entrance, where the greeting area, restaurants and stores are, I'm relieved to find the rent-a-car section not too far from there. I spot an familiar name car rental store front and head straight there.

"Okay, it will be fifty euros a day and you can return the car at anyone of our locations at the Costa Brava, or bring it back here on your departure day." The lady behind the counter says in an almost perfect English.

I start to take some money out of my bag when I hear someone behind me, "I'll take you there for free, miss." I turn around and see Biel standing there smiling down at me.

"Biel! How did you – when—" I start to say as I feel a big jolt in my stomach.

"Santi gave me the information for your flight. Come here!" He says and gives me a bear hug. Damn, he looks even better than I remember. "How are you?"

"I'm fine, fine, a little tired, but great. It's so good to see you, what a surprise!"

Biel tells the woman at the rent-a-car counter I won't need the car after all as he takes my suitcase and we make our way to his car. Driving out of the parking lot, he asks me how my flight went and I tell him about my dilemma in the Madrid airport, how I almost missed my flight. He laughs and tells me he's glad I made it. "I would hate it if you had to wait for me to come in the next flight." I tell him as we get onto a highway.

"Oh, I'm in no hurry, I would've waited for you, it's no problem!" He smiles at me and then turns back to the road.

I look around at the landscape and notice how different it is from the States, everything is so small. The highway itself is much narrower than our mammoth roadways back home. But it's so quaint and cozy.

"Is it far to your house?" I ask curiously.

"It's about two hours." He says casually.

"What? That long?" I say, suddenly feeling guilty that he had to drive all the way and back just to pick me up.

He turns to look at me and smiles. "I didn't have anything to do today, so I thought I would go for a ride. Really it's no problem at all."

As we drive I notice the change of scenery when we leave the highway. We start to go up the mountains and it's very green and pretty. Then, a while later I realize that the landscape is now different again and more dry looking with a lot of cactuses and different kinds of plants. It's so beautiful; then as we come around a curb there in front of us is a magnificent sight of the Mediterranean sea. It's a deep blue and with the light brown and green of the mountainous foreground it makes for an extraordinary picture.

"Beautiful, no?" He points ahead to the water.

"Wow…. It's really something." I say staring ahead, mesmerized.

Biel says that there's a different way we could've gone, which is almost straight up and quicker, but he thought I'd enjoy the scenery if we deviated and went through the mountains. I'm glad he went this way, it really is gorgeous and I can't help but get a feeling of glee being here with Biel in yet another beautiful part of the world.

"Remember last time we did something like this was in the Virgin Islands?" He says as if he read my mind.

I smile as I remember my favorite beach.

As we go in and out of curves the sea view comes and goes, until we reach the bottom of the mountain and go into a little town.

"If we go that way, we're in France in a few kilometers." He says pointing left. "And this town here is called Llança. We're going south a little to a very small town just passed Cadaques." He goes on to tell me that the town is so small that many people don't know it, it's hidden at the bottom of a small cliff and it's easy to miss from the road. We drive down a small road lined with Mediterranean pines overlooking the blue water, there are small cactuses all around the hills surrounding the road. We keep going down the road and when we turn the corner we come into a sign that reads 'Cova Blava', Biel says it means Blue Cave, named after a cave that's on the beach.

"You can only get in the cave during low tide." He explains and tells me that he thinks there are some prehistoric drawings all the way back in the cave, but it's hard to tell because they've been partly erased by the water and other elements. He thinks that there is not too much interest in having archeologists find out for sure because if they were this would turn into tourist hell and no one in the town wants that to happen. The town's Mayor insists that they are drawings from kids that made them many years ago.

We come into the town, which is absolutely adorable. There are small stores and apartments on top with colorful flowers abounding from their windows and terraces. Most people wave to Biel as he goes by. We drive through a few narrow streets and come onto a beautiful white house with red brick detail and a red tile roof with the blue sea right on it's backyard. It's three floors high and surrounded by a garden of pines, cactuses and green small bushes that look like wispy threads.

"This is my parent's house." He says as he stops the car in front. "But I'll take you to the 'Casa Teva' first if you like. I'm sure you want to rest a little, or change, take a shower…" He says the 'Casa Teva' is the name of the little hotel, or Inn, I'll be staying at.

"That sounds good, a shower and change of clothes would be great." I smile looking back at his house as we drive away. "That's a beautiful home."

"Well, you know you're welcome to stay there if you get tired of the hotel."

The 'Casa Teva' isn't too far down the street, in fact it's probably no more than a ten minute walk. If it wasn't for the turn in the road you could see it from Biel's house. Biel helps me bring my bags to the reception area and I sign in and get my keys. He says to call him whenever I am settled in and rested and with that he kisses me on both cheeks and drives back up the road to his house.

From my room, I have a perfect view of the blue sea. I have to say the 'sea' according to Biel because it's not an ocean, so I'm getting used to saying sea view instead of ocean view and I think I'm doing pretty good so far.

I take a shower with the intent of taking a little nap afterwards, but as I look through the window at the beautiful outdoor view I feel wide awake. It may be that I'm beyond the point of exhaustion so while I feel energized I'll take advantage of it. I call Biel at the number he gave me and ask if it's okay that I walk over to his house.

"Of course, you can come, are you sure you don't want me to pick you up?" He asks and I assure him I'll find the place alright and that some fresh air would be fantastic. I'm about to ring the bell by the front gate when it suddenly opens and Biel comes out of the house. He motions for me to come and leads me into the front door. The inside of the house is just as pretty as the outside, the furniture is modern but cozy and the rooms are very airy and bright. There are big French doors in the back of the house that lead to a swimming pool and right behind that there's the sea, right under the small cliff the house is perched on.

We come out to the pool where there's a few people sitting under an umbrella eating food from small plates on the table. Biel introduces his parents, Maria and Rafael, his brother Daniel and a couple of cousins and uncles. Biel says that he also has a sister who is out of town for a few days. They're all very friendly and invite me to eat 'Tapas' with them, which is the small plates of food they're eating that consist of things like olives, potatoes, squid, sausage pieces and a bunch of other stuff.

"How do you meet Biel, Sara?" Mateo, who is one of Biel's cousins, asks me as we sit by the pool a while later.

"Ah... well, I met him at the beach, where I live." I answer and go on to tell him the story. He tells me that when he finishes college he wants to go to New York. Marta, Biel's other cousin and Mateo's twin sister, also sits down with us and asks me a bunch of questions about America. To my surprise, they speak very good English, they say that in school they take pretty intensive language courses. They're about a couple of years younger than I, but are both still in school; taking a longer time to finish, as I did, except they are both going for their Master's. When Biel comes to bring me a drink I notice that it's almost night. I also notice that my speech is getting very slow and I'm starting to yawn. A lot.

"I think I'll be going back to the hotel soon." I say as I cover my mouth because of another yawn. "or I'll fall asleep right here on the pool deck!" They laugh and Biel offers to walk me back when I finish my drink. I say good bye to everyone and we make our way out of the house and down the road to the 'Casa Teva'.

"Thanks for walking with me." I tell Biel as we stop by the hotel's front door. He says to call him tomorrow when I'm up and we'll do something if I'm up to it. We stare at each other for a few awkward seconds and then he leans over to give me a kiss on each cheek. I know this is a custom here in Spain and everyone kisses everyone on both cheeks to say hello and good bye, but as his cheek brushed mine I felt a jolt inside and by the way he looked at me as he pulled away, I think he felt it too. I think. I mean, I am jetlagged and half asleep so I could be imagining things. Since it's all speculation, I leave it at that and concentrate on going up to my room and getting some sleep.

Twenty-three

"This is so good!" I say biting into a big calamari. Biel, Marta and I are at a restaurant by the beach eating lunch. I didn't wake up until passed twelve, but I could've slept like five more hours; the change of time really is harder to adjust to than I thought. But I also felt very hungry and when I called Biel he suggested going to eat lunch at his friend's restaurant. I thought it funny that everyone at the restaurant knew who I was before he even introduced me. Biel says the whole town knew I was coming, news here travel around in seconds specially due to the fact that everyone knows each other.

"Manel cooks everything himself from scratch." Biel says referring to his friend, the owner of the restaurant.

"And they are all recipes from his great grandmother." Marta ads as she also bites into a fat juicy calamari. Then, Manel comes over to our table and puts three more platefuls of food in front of us. He looks over at Biel smiling and then winks at me before walking away back to the kitchen.

After lunch we go back to Biel's house so he can show me his laptop commputer. Apparently he and Santi talked and Biel thought it would be easier for me to use his computer rather than lugging Santi's all across the continent. I talked to Mr. Halifax and told him I'd have his designs ready as soon as possible. Santi brings the computer into the kitchen and as he shows me how to get it going, Marta and his mom are animatedly talking in Catalan somewhere behind us.

"I use it almost everyday to send files to work." He explains, "But you can come to use it whenever you like."

"I don't want to be a nuisance, though… are you sure your family won't mind?" I say in a low voice, hoping he'll let me take the laptop to my hotel room if I need to.

"Oh, no, not my family!" He smiles, looking back at his mom and Marta, "They really like you, so don't worry, they will be happy to have you around." Marta and Biel's mother look and smile at me, and then keep talking. Oh, well I guess it's not so bad to work here, I could go by the pool, or the garden, the view is really inspiring.

"What do you say we go for a ride somewhere and I can show you the nice towns around here?" Biel says as he comes back to the kitchen after bringing the computer back in his room.

"I have to go meet David, actually, I am already late!" Marta says, "You guys go. We're still meeting later at Bule, no?" David is Marta's boyfriend, but I'm not sure what 'Bule' is.

"Bule is a little bar where we all meet on most nights." Biel says noticing my confused look. He then says something in Catalan to Marta before she smiles at me and says good bye running out the door.

"Let's go be tourists for a while then." Biel says as he takes out his car keys.

We say good bye to his mom and go into the garage where his car is parked. There we find his dad covered in grease, working on a small boat. Biel asks him something in Catalan and laughs and he looks over at me waving and tells me in a very heavy accent to have fun.

"He really wants to fix that boat." Biel laughs as he opens the car door for me to get in. "We've been working on it for days, but every time we fix something, we find another thing wrong." He says they probably should buy a new one, but his father is so old school that he'll try relentlessly to fix something before buying a new one.

"My dad is like that," I tell him as we drive out of the garage, "One time he worked on a television set for a month, when he was convinced he fixed it, he hit the 'on' button and it exploded!" He starts laughing so hard that he has to stop the car. Seeing him laugh like that makes me laugh too, so we're just sitting in the car like two idiots laughing hysterically. I can't remember the last time I laughed like this, it feels really wonderful. Then when we finally calm down I look through the windshield, I can't believe the beautiful sight of the blue sea sprinkled with sunshine.

"Wow, look at that." I say and we both get out of the car so I can get a good look. "It's just so incredible here... I love it!" Biel looks down at me as I look out to the water.

"I'm glad you're here, Sara." He smiles softly. I look up at him and get a flutter in my stomach.

"Me too." I look back towards the sea.

"Well, let's go then!" He says suddenly, "There's many things to see!"

It's almost two in the morning and I can't sleep. I keep going over the day's events in my head. It was an amazing day, Biel took me to so many gorgeous places that each place seemed more beautiful than the last. We took walks along some cliffs that overlooked the Mediterranean, went to a Castle from the Middle Ages propped on top of a cliff overlooking the sea. Biel says the name of the castle in Catalan is St. Peter of the Tire. When he told me this I went into another laughing fit and couldn't stop. We were having a drink at the bar in the Castle's entrance and the three other people in there where all looking at me very amused.

We also went to a fishing village where they had a fresh fish market in which the local fisherman sell their catch of the day to the public. Biel bought a big fish and some squid to make calamari for me since I like it so much. He put everything in a cooler with ice in the trunk. Then we took a walk around town and we got some 'churros' with chocolate that were to die for.

It's a pastry that vendors cook right there on their portable carts for you and you can eat them with sprinkled sugar or dunked in chocolate. It's a very popular treat all over Spain and when I tasted it I could see why.

Later in the evening when we came back we met Biel's cousins and friends at the Bule bar. I met Marta and Mateo's older brother, Xavier, or Xavi as they call him, who was very nice but sad because his girlfriend was in Germany for two months studying German. Apparently, according to Marta the real reason his girlfriend went away for a while was that she had been hinting marriage to Xavier and he wasn't responding, at least not positively. So she needed to get away for a while and set her feelings straight. Now Xavi was worried that she would come back and completely break things off.

"I think he realizes now that he does want to get married," Marta explained as we sat at a table in the back of the bar, "But thinks it may be too late. She won't call him back when he telephones her." She said that all their friends and family think they are perfect for each other and hope they can work things out. I saw Biel talking to Xavi by the bar for a while and he later told Marta and I that he would try to call Xavi's girlfriend in Germany to try and talk to her.

"She and Biel are good friends," Marta explained, "He'll try to convince her to give Xavi another chance.

Getting comfortable under the soft sheets, I keep seeing Biel's smiling face… I had so much fun with him… I had a really, really nice time…

I finally fall asleep while imagining Biel and I in a deep embrace on top of one of the cliffs we visited today. The bright blue sea behind us and Biel leaning down to kiss me... As I drift deeper into sleep I see Biel and I in a big fluffy bed kissing passionately, then as he kneels down to propose... and finally as I walk down the isle in a beautiful white dress towards him as he awaits for me at the altar of a church...

I wake up the next morning and I feel myself smiling, it's then my dreams come back to me as I blush under the covers. We're just friends, why am I dreaming these things? But I think deep down I feel myself liking him more than friends. Although, I can't tell what he feels himself, it's hard to tell. Sometimes I catch him looking at me in a certain way, that would indicate there is something there, but then he'll abruptly turn away or change the subject. It's as is he's deliberately avoiding anything that could lead to something more than friendliness. Still, it's just as well, I mean I don't know that I'm ready to start a relationship after what happened with Ivan.

Ivan. Wow, I haven't thought of him much lately. Come to think of it, I haven't thought of him at all before now. I have to wonder what it was I saw in him, when I compare him to Biel, there's just no... what am I doing? I shouldn't compare anyone to Biel, not unless, or until... Anyway, as I get dressed I recall that Biel went to Barcelona today for a meeting at his office there. He told me to go to his house anytime if I want to use his computer. I would've much have preferred to go to the beach,

which I haven't done yet, but being that it's overcast today
I'll take advantage and get some work done.

"That is very good!" A girl's voice from behind me exclaims. I
turn to see a girl of about my age with familiar features and also
with that pretty accent that most people who speak English have
here. I've been sitting outside by the pool under some trees
overlooking the water, it's still mostly overcast so it's not too hot.
In fact it's just perfect.

"Uh... thank you." I smile wondering who she is.

"Oh, sorry, I am Eva," She says as I stand up to face her.
"Biel's sister, you must be Sara, no?."

"Yes I am, nice to meet you." I tell her as we kiss each other's
cheeks, I'm still getting used to this, then she points back to the
computer screen.

"You are good, I like your style." She looks at Mr. Halifax's
brochure from a closer angle. I now recall Biel mentioning he had
a younger sister when I first met the family, but that she was on a
trip with friends. "My friend is also a Graphic Designer in
Barcelona." She says continuing to study the brochure.

"Biel told me you lived in Barcelona, right?' I say
remembering the conversation with Biel from the other day.

"Yes I do." She says nodding. "I'm on holidays now, so I will
be here for a few days. I just got back from Greece late last
night." She tells me about her trip with her friends and how she
loves that she has a month of vacation time for the summer.
That's something I wish we had back home, a whole month off!

"Okay, I will let you work." She starts to turn towards the house. "Maybe if the sun comes out later we can go swim." I nod and get back to the computer.

After a couple of hours I'm ready to take a break and just as I'm about to get up Biel's mom, Maria, comes out with a huge glass of what looks like Lemonade.

"For you." She manages to say in her very broken English. "Darink." And she mimics drinking from a glass then smiles.

"Thank you very much." I say and take a gulp. It's not exactly lemonade, but a lemony drink. It's pretty good actually a cross between lemon soda and lemonade. I'd like to say something to Maria, I feel strange just sitting here drinking as she stands by, but I know she won't understand a word I say. I feel relieved to see Eva coming out of the house and towards us so she can break the silence.

"Looks good!" She says pointing to the sun. "Do you want to come with me to the beach?"

"Sure! I'd love to!" I say, glad that I put on my bathing suit this morning, thinking that I could sneak in a swim sometime during the day. I shut down the computer and put it on the table under an umbrella and take the towel Eva has brought out for me. She says something to her mom in Catalan and then motions for me to follow her. "Have good time!" Maria calls after us.

We go down a little trail that comes right out off the end of the pool deck and leads onto a small beach area at the bottom of the small hill.

"Wow, I can't believe you have this beach right off your house." I say taking in the small little private beach. The next house also has a beach but it's separated by a rocky wall that leaves this area of beach all by itself. The other homes all share a bigger piece of beachfront that extends all the way down to my hotel and beyond which is where the town's public beach is.

"It is good, specially if you want to spend time by yourself." She smiles and adds raising her eyebrows a bit. "Many times I came with my ex-boyfriend, of course my parents come all the time so it's not exactly private… but it's nice if you want to have a quiet day."

"Sounds wonderful." I say as I lay down my towel and put some sunscreen on.

"Did you come with Biel down here yet?" She asks casually.

"Ah, no… I didn't, this is the first time I come to the beach since I got here a couple of days ago." I go on to tell her how Biel took me around to see the towns and areas nearby.

She turns to look at me. "You know, you're the first girl Biel has brought around to the house since…" She stops and looks down. "Since his last girlfriend." She looks up again, grinning.

I pause for a second not knowing exactly what to say to that and then, looking out to the water, I sigh. "Well… Biel and I are friends, you know, so I just came to see Spain and to visit him, as friends…"

"Ahh sure, friends." She says and wipes some sand off her towel, then looks straight at me, "You know… Biel has talked a lot about you."

For a moment I don't know what to say, but this comment sends a butterfly up my stomach. "Well…. We have become pretty good friends I guess." I finally add, knowing that I probably sound a little lame. To my relief just then Marta and Mateo come down the little trail to join us and the next thing we're all in the water splashing around. We stay at the beach until the sun starts to go down and it gets a little chilly. We pack our towels and things and go up the trail back to the house.

"You're coming for dinner, right?" Eva asks as I put the computer back in it's carrying case once we're back by the pool area.

"Uh… I don't know," I say not sure if I'm invited. "Is it okay with—"

"Sure! Of course." Eva says as her mom comes out from inside the house; she turns to her and says something in Catalan and Maria turns to me smiling.

"Si, yes, yes, you come eat." Maria says as she makes eating motions with her hand.

I tell Eva that I'll go to the hotel so I can shower and change and she says to be back by around nine thirty. She also says that Biel will be back by then from Barcelona.

Twenty-four

I'm putting some lip balm on when the phone rings in my room. Surprised because I'm not expecting anyone to call, I pick it up a little reluctantly.

"Uh, hola?" I say with a terrible accent. On the other end I hear a male voice laughing and realize it's Biel.

"Hey, you're learning!" He says still chuckling. "Listen, I'm here downstairs at your hotel, I thought I'd come pick you up if it's okay. Are you ready?"

"Y-yes, almost." Looking at my bare feet and choice of clothes laid out on the bed. "Why? Your sister said to be—"

"I know, I'm sorry… I was just going to the cellar to get some wine for the dinner and I thought I'd stop here and see if you want to come. It's on the way…"

"Well, sure I'd love to!" I say mentally trying to decide on one of the outfits. "Give me just five minutes and I'll be down." Hanging up, I realize I could've told him to come up so he doesn't have to wait standing around in the lobby, but oh well, I mean I'm just about ready to go.

The air feels mild as we walk down the street, it's so cool to go to a wine cellar for your wine! He says that they actually age the wine right there and it's all made by the owners of the cellar. They have a winery in another town where they grow the grapes, and bottle the wine and then they bring to the cellar and age it here.

"So, how was your day?" Biel asks as he takes down a big glass canteen of wine from the cellar wall. I tell him how I got a lot of work done on his computer and that I spent the afternoon at the beach with his cousins and sister.

"I'm glad you had fun." He says as he pays the lady at the register.

As we walk back up the street to his house I walk a little slower, right behind the houses is the sea and since there's pretty big spaces between homes you can get a good view of the water. I find myself wishing that we were going somewhere alone, just me and him, even if it's just walking on the street all night. I really like Biel's company and it feels nice to be with him.

We stop in front of a store that has a bunch of little stuffed fishes on the window. He tells me how as a boy he used to come here with his mom because she bought her stationary there. One day they went in he saw a cute small stuffed whale on the window. He asked his mom to get it for him, but she was in a hurry and said they'd get it next time. But he never saw that whale there again and always remembered it. AS he tells me this story I just find him even more adorable. I vow to myself to try and find this whale, I don't know how, but I'll try.

"Oh, shit, it's almost ten!" Biel says looking at his watch. "Let's go or they will eat everything!" He picks up the pace and I do the same to keep up with him. I guess it's the warm air and the atmosphere around that are making me feel all romantic and stupid. I brush away my thoughts and then from the corner of my eye I see some lightning off into the sea.

"I hope it won't rain tomorrow, I was thinking of going to the beach where the Blue Cave is." Biel says as we approach the gate to his house. "Would you like to go?"

When we get in the house everyone is sitting at the table about to eat. Eva looks up at us. "It's about time!" She exclaims, but then looks at me and winks. Great, I hope they haven't all been speculating about what Biel and I were doing... well, or not doing since we just went to get this wine and nothing else.

"More eat!" Maria says to me handing me a platter of chicken. I am so stuffed I could not eat a pea right now, so I just make heavy 'No' motions with my hands and pat my stomach. With that Maria turns to Biel and says something to him in Catalan to which he laughs.

"My mother says that you Americans don't eat anything, that you look like a tree trunk." He chuckles and Maria looks at me with an amused smile. I can't help but feel flattered, but with the five to seven extra pounds that I carry around, unless she means an Ent Tree trunk, I think she must be due for an eye check. But who am I to argue, I just smile humbly and say that everything was very good.

And a while later when dessert is served, I can't get away without having some Flan, to which I don't even try to decline because I love Flan. So I just stuff myself a bit more and resolve to walk a lot tomorrow when we go to the beach. When everyone is finished I help clear the table and try to help Maria with the dishes, but she firmly objects and sends me outside saying "Coffee soon."

A while later Biel and I are having some coffee by the edge of the cliff next to the trail that leads to the beach. It's so peaceful and serene with the gentle breeze hitting my face, I wonder what it must be like to live here. I'm looking out at some ship lights near the water's horizon when Biel's voice brings me out of my thoughts.

"It would be good if you stayed here, so you didn't have to leave to go back to your hotel." He says with a grin.

Not sure if he means that he's getting tired and wants to walk me back to the hotel and go to sleep, I get up and tell him I should be going. I don't want to be a burden, besides his family may want to relax and unwind and I'm in the way, I mean, it is almost one in the morning. Biel walks me back to the hotel and not wanting to hold him up too long I say a quick goodnight after we make plans for tomorrow's trip to the beach. Once upstairs in the room I get my stuff ready for tomorrow and climb into bed. I fall asleep going over the events of today and looking forward to tomorrow; I also find myself really looking forward to seeing Biel again.

Biel parks the car on a small parking lot overlooking the beach. His cousins wanted to walk over, but since we took a bunch of food and stuff to spend most of the day here, taking the car was more practical. The trip by car is longer, though, because we have to go by the road, whereas if we walked there's a trail that cuts through the cliffs and it's only about a fifteen minute walk from Biel's house. We each take something from the trunk and start to make our way down to the beautiful beach. Biel comes up next to me and takes an umbrella that's about to fall off my shoulder.

"Thanks." I smile and adjust my beach bag.

"The cave is down below that cliff there on the right." Biel says pointing to some rocks by the water. "You can only get in it when it's low tide." He says low tide should be around four, so we'll try to go in then.

"Who's coming to the water?" Marta says once we're all settled on the sand. Mateo and Biel both get up and follow her in. Not really feeling warm yet, I stay behind and just contemplate the surroundings. A while later Biel runs up to me from the water extending his hand.

"Come on! The water is great, come to swim!" I take his hand and let him lead me into the blue water. We swim and play around for a long time, we come out to eat lunch and then go back in again. The water is crystal clear and once you're in it feels great. We spend the rest of the day in and out of the water until we realize it's after four and decide to go venturing into the cave. To get to it we have to swim around the rocks and then come to a small beach in front of the entrance.

"This part gets covered by water at high tide and the cave also fills up," Marta says as we come onto the entrance. "So we have to be careful to be out before the water rises again."

"Let's go in." Mateo says and starts to enter the cave.

The ground is all sandy and it's about ten degrees cooler inside. The walls are damp at the entrance but less so as we get further in.

"Look at this!" Biel says as we go through a dark narrow tunnel and then come onto a large chamber that's strangely lit by a light above.

"How come it's light in here?" I ask looking around.

Biel points up towards the ceiling of the cave. "There's an opening up there, which is at the top of the cliff's grassy area." I look up and see a small hole in which I can just make out a little bit of blue sky. "Last year, a small boy fell through the hole and by luck he only broke his arm."

"They finally put a little fence around the hole so no one else can fall in." Marta laughs as she goes into another small tunnel. We all follow through another small chamber, this one is darker, but a bit of light still illuminates it.

"Wow, this is incredible!" I say taking in the smell of sea water and damp walls as I look into the chamber. I've never been in a cave before, so this is pretty amazing to me. I turn around and see Biel by the entrance watching me with a half smile. I then realize I must look pretty dorky being so awed by the cave, they must come in here all the time. I look at him and smile sheepishly walking towards him.

"It's nice, no?" He asks leaning back into the wall.

"Yes, I've never seen anything like this before." I say as I lean back against the wall next to him and look into the chamber again. He turns sideways towards me and suddenly I feel a flutter in my stomach as he gently touches my chin with his thumb. I shudder inside as I turn towards him. His face is very close to mine as I notice how the soft light makes his handsome features stand out. I smile nervously as he brushes my cheek with his hand and kisses me softly.

"Hello? Biel? Sara?" We both quickly pull away startled and see Marta coming through the short tunnel. "There you are! It looks like the tide is starting to come up, we should go." She says and turns back out of the tunnel. Biel smiles and winks at me as I look back at him with a stupefied look. He stops, then cups my face in his hands giving me a quick kiss and then grabs my hand leading me out of the cave.

The way back to the beach is like a blur. I'm in a daze by what just happened and almost feel like I imagined it, except I can still feel Biel's touch and a hint of his scent on my skin. We stay a while longer at the beach, but we pretty much play it cool, like a mutual understanding not to give ourselves away in front of his cousins. Well, not yet. I mean it's kind of new so I don't want to be like the lovey dovey couple all of a sudden.

Biel parks his car in front of the hotel and as we're getting my beach stuff out of the trunk, I notice some water coming down from my balcony and the one next to mine.

"That's funny," I say looking up. " I don't remember it raining today."

Biel follows my gaze and then stares at the water coming down. "That's not from any rain, it's really coming heavy."

Just then, the hotel owner comes running out the door towards us and starts frantically speaking to Biel in Catalan. She then turns to me with a very worried look on her face as Biel also turns to face me.

"She says that there's been a flood in the second floor." Biel says uneasily. "Your room is pretty full of water right now."

"Shit!" I can't believe this, of all the luck. "I'm going up to get my stuff." Biel says something to the owner and follows me into the hotel.

We get into the room and there's about four inches of water. Luckily the only things on the floor are a couple of pairs of shoes and they are just floating around, so I'm sure they'll dry out pretty soon. The owner lady comes into the room apologizing and I can tell she's mortified about this whole thing. She says something to Biel and then looks at me.

"She says she's very sorry about this, a pipe blew behind the wall." He explains. "And… she'll reimburse you and says you can stay in the downstairs room where she and her husband sleep."

"What? But… where will they sleep? I can't--"

Biel turns to the lady and says something in Catalan and she suddenly seems relieved.

"What's going on?" I ask him.

"Uh, well… if it's all right with you," Biel interrupts. "I told her you'd be staying with me, we have plenty of room at my house…"

The owner lady then says something else and smiles at me apologetically.

"She says that she'll let you know when everything is fixed and you can come back, at no charge."

"Uh… well, I guess that's fine." I tell Biel. "You're sure your mother and family won't mind?"

"No, of course not!" He smiles. "Here I'll help you get your things together."

We pack all my half wet stuff and head over to Biel's house.

The guest room is perfect. It has a huge window that leads to a balcony that looks over the beach down the cliff. His family is so welcoming, they were actually happy to have me stay, specially his mom. She was all smiles as she showed me to my new room. Biel said that when I got everything unpacked and in place, we'd go to the Bule bar for a drink with everyone else. Everyone else, I've learned, is just about anyone they know, who meets at the

Bule almost every evening before dinner. Not everyone goes everyday, but there's always someone there that they know.

When we get there most of the same people from the other day are there, I recognize Xavi right away and he looks even more depressed today. Poor guy, this girl must really be something. Too bad for him he didn't realize it before. We stay there for a couple hours talking to everyone and then they all agree to meet at a night club in the next town after dinner.

"It's a fun place to go." Biel explains when I ask him about the night club. "It's a typical summer place, it's in the open under a carp by the beach and it's always full of people."

"That sounds fun." I say trying to picture a place under a tarp being called a night club.

"Of course if you rather do something else… it's no problem with me." He smiles.

"Oh, no, no, I want to go!" I tell him. "I've never heard of a nigh club with a tarp in the open, I have to see this!"

"It's great, you'll have fun."

After a great dinner, Marta, Mateo, Eva, Biel and I get in Biel's car and head to the town up the road from us. It's a much bigger town than 'Cova Blava' and seems more touristy. We drive down towards the beaches and park the car by a gigantic tent. It's blue and covers a large area right next to the beach. The place is packed and we can hear the music from inside the car.

Once under the tent we go get drinks at the bar; not too much later we find ourselves all dancing within a huge crowd in the dance floor. After what seems like hours, Biel and I go to the bar to get some water, as I gulp my glass down, I notice Biel staring at me.

"More?" He asks and I nod laughing, he asks the bartender for another glass and turns to me again. "I never danced more than five minutes before, you're going to kill me!"

"It's good for you, keeps you healthy!" I smile at him as he hands me the second glass of water and I finish that one off too. "I'm having fun, this is fun."

"It is…" He leans over and kisses me. He pulls slightly back and just gazes at me half smiling. We then, at the same time, pull into each other and embrace into a kiss that just melts everything away. "You're like no other girl I met, there's something about you…" He says as he leans his forehead onto mine.

"This is…." I say not knowing what to say, but feeling elated. "It's like a dream – this, your family, your country… You." The rest of the night is like straight from a romantic movie; we dance, talk and spend most of the time in each other's arms. By the time we drive back home – at about four in the morning – Biel's cousins and sister pretty much have grasped the idea that we've hooked up. Luckily they all seem pretty okay with the fact, actually Eva has been giving me knowingly looks the whole ride back to their house.

"I had the best night with you." Biel says in a low whisper at the top of the stairs as we say good night. "I'm now wishing for your hotel room…" He snickers as he hugs me and we kiss for the hundredth time. I put my arms around his neck and hug him closer, we kiss again and then, reluctantly, I try to pull away a little.

"Okay, well I think we better go to sleep, or we'll wake up your whole family!" I whisper to him as I see his face smiling in the dim light. I'm so tempted to just go with him to his room, but I have to respect, and I guess admire, his mom's old fashion ways. I wouldn't want to disrespect her, she's a wonderful woman and besides, Biel and I have plenty of time together.

Later as I lie in bed, I feel myself drifting off to sleep feeling quite content just being with him, in his arms, by the moonlight... on the beach....

Twenty-five

The pounding of rain against the windows is what wakes me up the next day. I look at my watch and seeing that it's only nine thirty in the morning I go back to sleep for a while more. A few minutes later I hear a soft knock on the door and I groggily go to answer it, suddenly feeling a jolt picturing Biel standing outside the door.

"Good morning." Eva says in a low voice, as she stands right outside the doorway. "I hope I didn't wake you… it's after eleven, so I thought you might be awake."

"Oh… yes, I'm awake." I say unconvincingly as I look at my watch. It certainly is passed eleven… I must have really fallen asleep after I first woke up with the rain. I motion for her to come in trying not to look as asleep as I feel.

She smiles and walks in looking towards the terrace windows.

"It's really raining!" She says and sits on the edge of the bed. "I think it will be like this all day, so we'll probably have to be in the house all day…"

"I don't mind resting after last night! We danced for hours…."

Eva smirks. "I know…" She nods, still smirking. "So you are… more than friends now, you and Biel, no?"

"Well… I guess we would be, yes." I blush and giggle.

"I am very happy." She looks me in the eye and pats my arm. "After his last girlfriend… well it's good to see him happy again with someone." She stands and walks to the terrace doors. "Actually, since he's been back from USA, he has mentioned you a lot. He even told my grandmother about you while she was sick, and she was sorry not to be able to meet you because she went away on vacation right before you arrived." She turns and looks at me smiling warmly.

"I would've liked to meet her too, Biel has talked a lot about her." I get a great feeling inside as Eva tells me all this. We talk a while more and then she says that Biel has gone to get us some breakfast.

"In this rain?" I ask, looking outside. "Poor guy!"

We go downstairs and Biel is already there, all soaked but he managed to keep all the breakfast bags completely dry. He brought croissants, fresh bread and all kinds of pastries that I've never seen before and they all look delicious. We take our time eating and drinking coffee while the rain continues to pour outside. When we're finished, I ask Biel for the computer, figuring this is a good time to try and finish those designs.

I can't help but realize that I only have two more days before I have to go back to the states and to reality. Biel still isn't sure when he'll get back, but he says he's been working hard to finish the project they got him started on while he's been here so that he can go back. He says tomorrow morning he has to go to Barcelona for a meeting and he'll find out exactly what day he can return to Florida.

"I think I can have everything finished here in about two weeks." He says as he hands me his laptop. I'm sitting on a bench by his bedroom window looking out to the grayish sea as the rain continues to fall.

"Thanks." I smile as I take the computer, I turn to look outside again. "I will miss this place… it's so pretty, even when it's raining."

Biel moves the laptop over on the bench and sits next to me, running he hand through my hair. "Like you." He says. I turn to face him and he caresses my cheek and kisses me, I kiss him back and we embrace deeply. He hugs me even closer and I feel a jolt up and down my spine; we're kissing pretty heavily when his bedroom door suddenly opens. We pull apart as we awkwardly look at Eva standing by the doorway blushing, obviously embarrassed, but still smiling under her breath. I fix an invisible piece of hair and pull the laptop towards me as I smile stupidly.

"Very sorry… sorry, I… sorry." She then says something in Catalan as she closes the door softly. Biel and I stare at each other, also a little embarrassed, but then we bust out laughing. He plants a quick kiss on my lips and stands up taking the laptop from the bench. He holds out his hand and helps me to stand up.

"We should stop probably..." He looks at me knowingly. "Or next time it will be my mother coming in and who knows where she will find us, no?" He laughs, but right before opening the door he turns to face me once more and hugs me with one arm as he holds the laptop with the other and whispers in my ear. "I don't know what you do to me, Sara." I shudder at those words, feeling the same about him; a big smile forms on my face as I follow him out of his room.

We spend the rest of the rainy day in the living room. Me with the laptop doing Mr. Halifax's designs, Biel doing work for his job and Eva reading a book. Every so often I steal a look at Biel, a couple of times he has noticed and just gives me this cute smile and wink. I try to stretch this day as long as possible since my time here is coming to an end. After dinner Biel and I go for a walk on the beach, we talk about all kinds of stuff and laugh, man this guy can make me laugh! We end the evening with an incredible make-out session right by the water's edge. I'm just about to fall asleep curled up in his arms when we realize the time and start to make our way back to the house.

"Good night." He says as he hugs me in front of my bedroom door. "You're like... una flor venenosa."

"I'm what?" It sounds romantic, whatever it is....

He laughs and looks at me mischievously. "A... poison flower."

I punch him in the arm and he laughs even more.

"Shhh! You'll wake everyone!" I wishper, but start laughing when I see his comedic expression.

We say good night for the tenth time and then he tells me that he'll see me in the afternoon when he gets back from his meeting in Barcelona. I almost forgot that he won't be here in the morning and as I walk into my room I feel a little guilty that I kept him up so late. Although it was a wonderful night, I feel bad that he won't get much sleep; I hope he'll be fine for his meeting... I fall asleep longing for tomorrow afternoon and wonder what we'll do. Heck, I could sit there and count rocks with him and have the best time of my life.

As small as this town is, I never thought I could get lost in it. I've been looking for the paper store for like an hour. Eva gave me pretty good directions, but I think I've wandered off the path a long time ago. Every time I see an interesting shop I turn in that street thinking that I can just retrace my steps, but I think I re-retraced my steps so many times that I've completely got off the loop all together. Oh well, I figure I'll find my way eventually, some streets are starting to look familiar because I've probably been walking in circles for a while now.

A sweet smell gets my attention and I follow it to a little bakery tucked into a small corner of the street I'm on. I start to make my way to see what smells so good when a familiar sound makes me look. I can hear someone speaking English, not American English, but a clear British English. I see two girls speaking animatedly at the store front next to the bakery. It's a chic clothing store and the two girls are standing next to a sales rack that's been put out on the sidewalk.

I'm about to go passed them and into the bakery, when I hear something that makes me stop. One of the girls is beaming and is nodding excitedly.

"I knew Biel would do it!" One of the girls says, the one without the British accent. Actually, as I look at her from behind another sales rack on the sidewalk a little closer to the store I realize that she looks quite familiar. I met her the other night at the bar, she's one of Biel's cousin's friends, I think her name was Sonia. I'm about to go say hello when I suddenly stop as the British girl responds to her.

"I know... I can't believe he proposed! I thought we were over for sure. Biel is really wonderful." The British girl is gushing to Sonia. I feel a deep pang in my stomach as I try to hunch behind the rack so the girls don't see me.

"I'm so glad things worked out, you guys are perfect for each other. You know," Sonia says as she puts a hand on her arm. "He was sulking for months after you left him!"

"Really?" The British girl has a smile from ear to ear. "Oh... I was so devastated also, but I had to show him that I meant it, I needed to know we had a future, or I had to move on."

"Well, Biel..." Sonia starts to say, but I can't listen anymore... I back away from the rack trying to go unnoticed, but I almost trip on it as I start to walk away.

"Sara?" I hear Sonia's voice call after me, but I just keep walking. I'm not sure which direction I'm going, but I need to get away. Away from here, away from Biel's friends, Biel's house, Biel's town. Away from Biel.

I finally find his house after what seems like hours walking around these now claustrophobic streets. I go to my room and pack everything up, I just stuff everything into my suitcase as fast as I can and make my way out, hoping not to run into any members of Biel's family. As I get out of the front gate I think I see Maria from the corner of my eye coming out of the front door. But I don't look, I just keep on walking down back to the hotel. Luckily the rooms are all cleaned up and dry, the owner called yesterday to let me know I could return, but Biel told her I'd be staying at his house for the rest of my trip.

When I walk into the lobby the owner's husband, Pere, is at the front desk and looks at me a little strange. I try to act natural as I ask for my old room back. Luckily he's able to make out what I'm saying and he punches something into the computer and hands me the keys, smiling warily. I force a smile back and taking the keys I quickly make my way to the elevator. Finally, I'm locked in my room, safe and away from everyone. When I see my face in the mirror I can understand Pere's bizarre looks towards me. My face is tear stricken, red and swollen. I look like complete hell - exactly how I feel.

Somehow I manage to make arrangements with a cab company to come pick me up and take me to the airport. With my little dictionary it took me less than a half hour to finally make myself understood. The problem is that today is some kind of Holiday in Catalonia and the earliest I can get a taxi is at six tomorrow morning. I try to read to pass the time, but I can't concentrate and I can't get rid of the huge sickening knot in my stomach.

I set the alarm clock for five in the a.m. and try to sleep. I put my headphones on so that I can escape all this and block out any noise, or any possible knocks on the door from Eva or anyone from Biel's family. I just can't face them right now. Or ever. I don't know how much they know of his rekindled love, or whatever the hell it is, with this British girl, but I'm sure they'll be happy to learn he has come to his senses. They will just want to comfort me and tell me what a nice girl I am and how sorry they are it turned out like this, but hey hope I can remain friends, blah, blah, blah. Right. Bullshit.

I drown into a deep sleep and have vivid dreams about these last few days, except they are full of images of a wedding in which Biel and the British girl are married by a dolphin named Niko who can talk. Niko asks the British girl where I am and she says I am eating cakes by the wine store and that I have the rings so someone has to come get me. Biel's mom, Maria, comes to get the rings just as I'm taking the last bite of cake. When I swallow I feel something sharp scratch my throat and I realize I swallowed the rings. Maria starts to yell at me and say I eat too much.

She runs towards me and starts hitting me with a live fish, I'm yelling and crying and all of a sudden I sit up and find myself on the hotel bed, all sweaty with my heart beating a hundred miles an hour. I look on the bedside table and reach over to turn off the alarm clock. I feel horrible, but relieved that it's time to wake up, get ready and the hell out of here.

An hour later I'm showered and packed as I waiting by the window for the taxi. When I see him pull up I make my way downstairs drop the keys off and say goodbye to Pere, who is half asleep behind the desk; I feel bad he had to get up just for me, but I'm sure he'll go right back to sleep.

The ride back to Barcelona is sad and nostalgic as I remember these last few days, which truthfully have been amazing. It's hard to believe I'm now in the back of a taxi feeling so alone and not to mention completely deceived. I dread what lays ahead which is a four hour wait at the airport and then once in Madrid another three hour wait followed by the long nine hour flight back to Miami.

It's not until we're taking off the Barcelona runway that I realize I never emailed the designs to Mr. Halifax. I don't even have printouts of them. Everything is in Biel's laptop all finished up but without a chance of ever being seen by anyone other that maybe Biel, if he bothers to look at them before he puts them in the little trash icon and hits 'empty trash'.

"Shit." The lady next to me gives me a look before I realize I've said it out loud, I sigh and hold back the tears. Well, there goes my job and my only potential customer.

Twenty-six

"You've got to call him, Sara." Courtney says as she cooks some of her famous eggs. She picked me up at the airport a while ago and as soon as I saw her at the passenger pick up area I busted out crying. I couldn't help it, I really didn't want to make a scene in public and thought I could wait until we were in the car, but as soon as I saw her, I just lost it. I was so miserable through the whole long trip not able to talk or let all these miserable feelings out, that one look at my trusted best friend just filled me with relief and sadness at the same time.

"You have to get those designs to Mr. Halifax, I'm sure Biel will email them to you."

"I can't. I just can't." I say firmly. "I can't even think about anything that happened over there." Even the designs remind me of him. I mean I'm sure my inspiration was in part due to just being with him. You know how they say that when you are happy or in love your imagination just soars. Damn, did I say in love? Was I in love with him? Is that why I'm so miserable? That bastard. God I hate him.

"But Sara—"

"How… how's Santi? How are you and him?" I ask suddenly remembering the night at the convention, when he and that woman…

"We're good." She smiles faintly. I can tell they are more than good by the way her eyes light up as she hears his name. I just hope he's not like his friend, I'm definitely going to be keeping an eye on him. Although from a distance, specially when Biel comes back, because I don't plan on being anywhere near him. Of course, now that he's 'engaged' – emphasis added – he may not even come back; with Ms. Britain professing her love for him at the altar, why would he want to go thousands of miles away? "We're doing okay, but listen, you can't throw this away. I'll call him for you if you want."

"No!" I exclaim. "No. Listen I'll figure something out. Tomorrow I'll call Mr. Halifax and explain. I'm sure I can recreate the designs I did. I mean I just did them a few days ago, they won't be hard to redo." Frankly, I'm not sure I can. But right now I want all contact cut out with Biel, I feel humiliated and hurt and miserable… I just can't even think about him.

I eat half an egg and try to finish it, but I don't have an appetite. Later, as I lay in bed images of Cova Blava flood my mind, I try to push them away but the more I try the more I remember my time there. Tired as I am I cannot fall asleep so I just toss and turn not being able to shake the awful ache in my chest.

When morning finally comes I drag myself to work, not wanting to face anyone there either. As I go up in the elevator, I try to play in my mind what I'll say to explain the lack of designs for Mr. Halifax. I'm even more worried about explaining to Mr. Halifax himself why I don't have anything for him. He took the chance of relying on me and told Amy and Neil that he would work only with me. As hard as they tried to convince him that they would do the work for him while I was away he would not hear it. And now, I've let him down and I'll never hear the end of it from Neil and Amy; well, I probably will hear the end of it, the end of me working here, that is.

Marcia is as friendly as always when I walk by, hardly looking up to say hello. I'm halfway through the hallway walking towards my closet-office when she calls after me.

"Neil wanted me to give you this." She hands me a sheet of paper, I look at it and see a list of coffees on it. "He'll need them right away, some new clients are coming in a half hour."

I walk away without answering her, wondering if I'd be good behind a coffee counter. I sure have enough experience with coffee.

I'm putting the coffee in the conference room when I hear someone clearing their throat behind me.

"Hello Sara." Amy's unfriendly voice says. I turn to see her sneering. "What took you so long with the coffee, the clients are already here."

"Well, it's here now!" I say beaming at her.

"I need to see you in my office when this meeting is over. I'll come get you when I'm done here."

"Sure. I'll be in my closet!" I say and glide out of the conference room leaving her there staring after me. I don't know why I said that, but something in me just feels indifferent to everything, specially to everything in this ridiculous job.

A couple of hours later I'm sitting facing Amy in her office, I've just told her that I don't have the designs, and she can go ahead and call Mr. Halifax to let him know if she so pleases.

"Well, I certainly will call him." She says with such superiority you'd think she was the Queen of the West. "but not before I say a few things to you."

"Oh? And what things would those be?" I say folding my arms expectantly.

She stands up and walks around her desk to where I'm sitting.

"You've proven yourself completely incompetent. You can't even get the coffee right." She pauses. "And your design skills are substandard. We thought we could take you in and train you and maybe help you along in your career, but with your attitude that really seems an impossibility.

We give you the chance to do something for an important client and you've completely let us and him down. Now what, we'll look absolutely unprofessional all because of your inability to do anything." She sighs deeply before continuing. "And worst of all, you really thought that by whoring yourself to Brian he'd really help you get up in this company. That's just disgusting and pathetic, really, girls like you don't get anywhere." She's practically yelling now and hasn't noticed that the door has opened and there's a group gathered outside listening in.

I sigh deeply and as if a force inside me is in control I stand up to face her.

"Listen you hypocrite, I'm not the one who offers herself to other people's clients so she can work on their campaigns." As I say this her snug expression slowly turns into one of alarm. "Yes, that's right I know how you offer sex favors to clients so they'll give you their accounts. How about Mr. Rollings? Neil's client whom you wanted for yourself to prove that he preferred you to Neil? Except that what he preferred was what you provided for him, wasn't it?"

There's silence for a few seconds.

"How – you can't know this! Who said–?

"Let's just say word got around at the convention." I smirk at her. "Also, let me tell you that I never even as much as touched Brian; he kept asking me out until I finally agreed and only so I could get some information out of him. And some information I got, let me assure you!"

"Is this true?" We turn and see Neil standing there biting the earpiece of his glasses with his head cocked to one side staring at Amy. Behind him are Larry, Marcia and making his way in Mr. Tivoli. "You did... that to get clients? No wonder..." He chuckles. "I never thought much of your design talent."

"Shut up Neil." Mr. Tivloi says as he approaches me. "By the way, Sara, Mr. Halifax loved your designs he wants all of them, he couldn't pick just one." He smiles softly as I stare at him not sure I heard right. "Now if I'm correct, the information you got from Brian is that this department has been hiring junior designers to be gophers, which would explain the quick turnover; four junior designers in one year. I thought something wasn't right. I'm also disappointed that my son was involved in helping with this."

"That's really terrible Mr. Tivoli." Neil says as he folds his arms looking grave.

Mr. Tivoli looks at him and shakes his head sighing.

"As for you Amy." Mr. Tivoli turns to her making a face. "That's quite dismal of you, really, I suggest you seek different work. I'd offer you a clerical position downstairs but there's no one there you could proposition to get ahead." Larry lets out a laugh and then disguises it as a cough as he looks on amused. Amy is looking down towards the floor and seems to be sinking down an inch by the second. She suddenly picks up her purse and starts grabbing things from her desk dropping half of them as she makes her way down the hallway.

"Amy?" Neil calls after her poking his head out of Amy's office door. "Uh, we could probably work something out, I'm open to any offerings you might have…"

He turns back to face us and looks at Mr. Tivoli. "I, well… I could train her a little on how to design better, you know?"

"I'm sure you could." Mr. Tivoli smiles at him. "You should hurry after her and please take your things on the way out. I don't have space for such ethics here."

"Excuse me?" Neil says authoritatively and stares at him. "You can't do that, I run this department, without me this will all go to shit. You, you need me, I'm a great designer, I--" Now he's panicky and desperate.

"Good bye Neil." Mr. Tivoli walks out of Amy's office and motions for me to follow him. Behind me is Neil whom I see going into his office mumbling to himself.

I'm still trying to figure out if Mr. Tivoli actually said what I heard. How did Mr. Halifax get a hold of the designs?

"First, I want to apologize for this mishap with the so called… Junior position, is it?" Mr. Tivoli says in his office as he hands me a glass of coke and sits down on the couch across from me. "I should've been aware of this, but as I'm getting ready to retire, I wasn't paying much attention and I thought things were being handled by my son." He chuckles.

"Your son will be in charge?" I ask not being able to hide the disbelief in my voice.

He grunts and takes a sip of his grape juice. "I know… thing is, he's able to do it and I thought if I let him to it he'd grow up."

Apparently Mr. Tivloi has been extending Brian's authority over this last few years to get him in the right mode for the responsibility. He's obviously been giving him too much credit. But he insists he is capable, if he could only stop being led by his pants. Yes, he actually said that.

"If only he'd meet the right girl…" He looks straight at me.

"Uh, Mr. Tivoli I—" I start to say shaking my head.

His eyes widen, and then he smiles. "No, no, no… I just meant a girl like you, you know someone who will straighten his caboom right up." He sighs and leans back on the couch. "Unfortunately for him, I think there's already someone who's snatched your attention…" He grins.

I forgot that Biel knows Mr. Tivoli, I wonder if he's aware of Biel's new found fiancée. "Well… that's no longer the case. I don't think it's going to happen." I say not wanting to divulge into this subject, specially not with Mr. Tivoli.

He purses his lips and gives me a sideways glance. "Mmm." Is all he says. We sit in silence for a few seconds and then he tells me that I'm welcome to stay at my job, as a real Graphic Designer. He also tells me that he won't retire right away, that he wants to make sure Brian is up for the job, so he'll stick around while he mentors him.

"I'd get bored not working anyway. The wife and I can go on vacation anytime we want, I don't have to be retired to do that."

We sit and talk for a while and I realize that he is a pretty nice person, you know like a dear grandfather. He is, however, pretty smart, much more than he lets on. But I think that's just part of how he operates, that way he's able to be on to things before anyone suspects anything. He just hasn't been using his MO lately and it led to the deterioration of the Art Department. Of course, Brian himself is to blame for that, since he's the one that made the Junior stint possible for Neil.

After my talk with Mr. Tivoli I ask him if it's alright that I go home early. The jetlag is really catching up with me and not having slept a wink the night before I'm just about ready to drop. I'm very relieved when he says to go ahead and take tomorrow off as well. All I want to do is fall onto my comfortable bed.

Twenty-seven

When I walk into the apartment Courtney and Santi are on the couch giggling and when I shut the front door they abruptly stop. I walk into the living room and see two wide pairs of eyes peering from behind the couch's backrest and I realize I've interrupted something. Of course, they weren't expecting me so early.

"Carry on!" I sing as I walk straight to my room and close the door. Feeling like I'm forgetting something I suddenly realize that I never asked Mr. Tivoli where Mr. Halifax got the designs from. It doesn't make any sense, I could've sworn I never emailed them, but my brain is too foggy to try and figure it out now. I take my shoes off and lay down on the bed sighing with absolute relief.

Not five minutes go by when there's a soft knock on the door.

"Yes?" I say, my voice hardly coming louder than a whisper.

Courtney opens the door slowly and walks over to the bed.

"Hey." She says as she sits on the edge. "How come you're home so early? Is everything okay?" I sit up and look towards the door.

"Where's Santi? I'm sorry I interrupted…"

"Oh, don't worry about it, he had to go anyway. We were just wrestling around." She blushes slightly. "Besides, I think something's up… You wanna talk about it?"

Truth is I really want to tell her everything, even if I'm dead tired and can't talk without slurring. I prop up my pillow and she sits crossed legged in front of me as I go on to tell her the day's highlights. She specially gets a kick out of what I said to Amy.

"I can't believe she acted so high and mighty after what she did at the convention…" Courtney shakes her head.

"She evidently did it all the time." I laugh and then look down, remembering it was Biel who told me all this.

"Nasty slut." She says.

"Looking back at it, it's almost funny, isn't it?" I say. "It's almost like something right out of a TV drama." I laugh.

"So, you're gonna stay there then?"

"Well, for now I guess." I look out the window towards the ocean. "I'm not sure what I want to do. I'd like to eventually do freelance work, you know, work for myself make my own hours."

"You should." She affirmed.

"I know, but it's hard, I mean I'd have to build a client base and all that. I have to think about a lot of things before I can do it." I imagine myself working from the apartment watching the ocean as I create some great design for an important company. Going for a swim whenever I needed inspiration.

"Sara… and, uh, Biel?" She asks reluctantly. "Have you heard from him at all?"

I feel a pang on my chest as the visions of freelance heaven disappear with a poof. "No. And, honestly, I don't think I will. I mean he's probably busy planning his wedding."

"Listen, about that…" She starts. "Santi and Biel are pretty good friends, right?"

"Yeah, so?"

"Well, you'd think he would know about this British fiancée person…"

"He probably does, but he wasn't going to tell on his good friend, now was he?" I'm finding myself wanting to lay back down and forget this conversation as soon as possible.

"No, he doesn't." She looks me straight as I try to avoid her gaze. "He doesn't know about any other girlfriend of his, other than the one who dumped him last year. And it can't be her."

"Why not? Maybe it is her."

"She wasn't British, and how would it make sense, if she dumped him, why would he have to persuade her to get married? They weren't even on any speaking terms. Besides, she lives in Barcelona and isn't in any friendly terms with any one at the beach town."

I'm too tired to make sense of anything. "Look, I'm just going to sleep for a while, I'm dead tired." I give her a half smile. "We'll talk more later, okay?"

She sighs, but gets up off the bed and walks towards the door.

"Court?" I call after her. "Thanks, you know… for listening and everything." She smiles and walks out of the room closing the door behind her.

I manage to fall asleep because I'm so beat. But, I still wake myself up as I toss and turn dreaming strange things. I'm in a cave by a beach, being chased by a giant green lizard who makes loud patter noises. Then I'm in Neil's office listening to him give a speech about design skills as he balances himself on a chair with one leg. Then Amy walks in with a tambourine tapping on it as she asks Neil to let her have her way with him.

There's a knocking noise that comes from Biel's mother beating on a skillet calling everyone to dinner as the tapping gets louder I wake up. Still feeling tired I turn on the bed and fall asleep again to find myself sitting on an empty beach with a huge cliff behind me. I feel peaceful until I see a figure emerging from the water and realize it's Biel. Of course he's looking gorgeous and I hate myself for not being able to take my eyes off him. He approaches me and kneels by me as he starts to kiss me. I force myself to push him away and as he pulls himself back looking hurt, I see a pelican thumping on a rock with its beak. He leans in again and I yell 'No!", stand up and start to run down the beach.

All of a sudden I open my eyes and can't tell if I'm awake or asleep. I hear a pounding noise and look around for the pelican, instead I just see my room and then my eyes fall on my alarm clock. 12:29 pm. Wow, I really slept long. My concentration is broken when I hear the pounding noise again and realize that it's someone knocking on the door. I stand and walk over to open it.

"Sorry to wake you." Courtney is standing there with a funny look on her face.

"What's wrong?" I say alarmed.

"Well... before I tell you, promise you won't do something stupid."

"Why, what's going on?" I say wondering what's up.

"Come and look." She says in a low voice. She points to the couch. "Shhhh, he's sleeping."

I look and freeze on the spot as I see Biel sleeping peacefully on the couch. Damn, I forgot how handsome he was. Coming back to my senses, I stare at Courtney. "What the hell is he doing here?"

"He came hours ago." She says still whispering, and walks back towards my room. "He said he needed to talk to you and I told him you were sleeping. So he said he'd wait until you woke up."

"Why didn't you tell him the truth? That I don't want to see or talk to him." I tell her as I my head fills with memories of my time with him in Spain just days ago. I feel my eyes fill with tears as the hurt comes all over again.

"Listen, Sara." She grabs my hand and makes me sit down on my bed. "While he was here we talked. A lot. He told me about this British girl, the whole thing."

I stare at her. "So, what, he came to apologize and to invite us to their reception?" I say fuming.

"No, you idiot!" She flares her eyes at me and I can see her trying not to laugh. "You have it all wrong. He doesn't have any fiancée."

"Then who was it I saw? I heard what she said."

"Yes you did." She sighs deeply. "Listen, Biel will tell you. He wants to tell you. I mean the guy waited hours for you to wake up, I finally told him to knock on your door, but nothing, not a peep out of you. He didn't want to wake you, so we waited a while more, I went to do some laundry and the poor guy fell asleep waiting for you to get up."

"This is crazy." I say. We sit there in silence a couple of seconds when a voice on the doorway makes us look.

"Hi." Biel says leaning on the door not daring to come in.

"Hello." I say a little awkward.

"Come on. Come with me, I want to talk with you." He says gently holding out his hand.

Courtney pushes me off the bed and I give her a look, but smile at her despite myself.

"Go." She says as she motions for me to go. "I'll make something to eat, you guys hungry?" Without waiting for an answer she goes to the kitchen.

Biel and I go out to the beach and walk in silence for a few minutes.

"I heard Mr. Halifax really liked the designs you did for him." Biel says looking at me sideways.

"Yes he..." Wait a minute. I look at Biel and smirk. "Of course, you sent them to him, didn't you?"

He nods. "I thought you would have figured that already..."

"Well... I thought about it, but..." I say feeling kind of dumb. I mean the files were in his computer and nowhere else.

"So, what were you dreaming about?" He asks as we reach the shore.

"What?"

"When you were sleeping earlier." He smiles. "I could hear you from the living room yelling 'no' a lot."

I glare at him. "Really? I can't imagine about what..."

As we walk I realize how much I've missed his cute accent and the way he talks; I guess I've basically just missed him all together. Suddenly, Biel stops walking and faces me. "Listen, Sara... Those few days you spent with me in Spain were incredible for me."

I look up at him expectantly and wait for him to go on.

"When you left I..." He looks towards the ocean and back at me.

"Who was that British girl?"

There's silence for a few seconds.

"That was my friend Claire." He says and then smiles. "Xavier's girlfriend."

I stand there looking at him not sure what this means. "You mean the girl he was so bummed out about? What do you and her—"

"She asked me to talk to him to try to convince him to propose to her. That's why she left, she got tired of the relationship not going anywhere, but she couldn't be without him. So I had some good talks with him and from what you heard, it worked."

I look up at him and feel a rush of affection for him and at the same time I feel like a fool.

"Okay, I feel stupid now." I say turning my head down kicking a rock around with my foot. I'm so embarrassed, what must his family think of me. I just took off without saying good-bye or anything, how rude was that. They probably won't want to see me again. "I didn't mean for things to go like this."

"I know..." He says and looks at me gravely. "Listen, Sara... I realized something after you left and that's what I need to talk to you about."

"What is it?" Something in the tone of his voice doesn't sound good.

"Well... when you left suddenly like that, it made me remember how I felt with, how I felt when—"

"When your last girlfriend left you?" I finish for him.

He nods. "I'm not ready for that again." He looks straight at me. "I just need some time and I'm so sorry that I let myself go with you in Spain. I tried not to, but it wasn't possible." He reaches and touches my cheek. I take a step back and turn my face away. I think this is almost worse than overhearing the British girl.

"Sara, I am sorry and I do love you. I hate to do this but the chance of losing you and going through that agony again is something I can't think of right now."

"Sure, you can't lose what you don't have…" I say faintly as my stomach turns.

He bites his lip and grabs my hand. "I hope you can be around when I can get my shit together, but I understand if you won't." He leans closer and almost whispering says he's sorry again.

I pull away and shake my hand lose from his, trying to hold back the tears I feel coming.

"I'm sorry too, Biel. Sorry that this is how you deal with life, avoiding any chance of something good because it's easier." I hear myself saying. "Love means risk, I don't see how you can say you love me." I tell him and start to walk back to the apartment before I say something more I'll regret.

"Sara…" I turn and see him standing there, as handsome as ever, unfortunately for me. I gather my courage and face him again.

"I got dumped on too, Biel, but for you I'd take the chance." I shrug my shoulders as he stands there just watching me. "Goodbye, Biel." I quickly turn around and start walking fast this time not being able to hold the tears in.

Twenty-eight

It's been three days since the last day I saw Biel on the beach and I can't stop reliving it in my head. I try to concentrate on work but it just keeps coming back. Trying one more time to come up with a concept for a brochure I'm struggling to design, I'm startled by a voice on my phone's intercom.

"Call for you on line two. I think she said her name is Courtney or something." By the tone of her voice I can tell how much Marcia is hating it. Ever since the showdown with Neil and Amy she's had to actually do her job and put calls through to my office.

"What's up?" Courtney's voice says on the receiver. "Hungry?"

I look at my watch and see that's it almost one.

"Yeah, I guess." I lie as I'm not hungry at all, but I could use a break. "Where do you want to meet?"

A while later we sit at a cozy restaurant on Las Olas that's nearby to both her store in the mall and my office building.

"Hey, how come we've never been in here before?" I ask noticing how cute this place is. Courtney, however, doesn't respond as she is looking intently behind me over my shoulder. I turn around and follow her gaze and quickly turn back as I see what she's staring at. Or who. It's Ivan.

She leans over towards me. "Maybe because lawyers like to hang out here?" She cocks her head sideways and purses her lips.

"Just look at the menu and pretend you didn't see him." I say as I, myself, try to look occupied with the daily specials. "Maybe he won't see us."

"Too late." She whispers keeping her head down, almost kissing the menu.

"Sara?" I hear a familiar voice and look up to find Ivan next to our table. He has the goofiest smile I've seen on anyone's face. "How are you?"

I manage a weak smile.

"Gosh, I've missed you!" He says crouching down next to my chair.

"Really?" I say as over exaggerated as I can.

"Where's uh... what was her name? Did she dump you for a real lawyer yet?" Courtney blurts out and I almost choke on my water.

He is quiet for a second. "Eve? Um, no we're no longer together." He says and turns his attention back to me. "Hey Sara, we should get together sometime."

I gaze at him not believing he's serious. "Uh, I don't think so, Ivan." I look at Courtney and she's shaking her head in disbelief.

"If you don't mind, we need to order so we can get back to work." Courtney makes a shoo motion for him to take a hint.

"I'll call you... okay sweets?" Ivan says as he slowly gets up and starts to walk back to his table.

"Whatever." I mumble and look at Courtney.

"Sweets?" She says once he's out of earshot. "What a moron."

"Amazing." I sigh. "Men can be really amazing."

We order our lunch, me a fish dip appetizer, Courtney a chicken sandwich, then as soon as the waiter walks away Courtney sighs and looks straight at me.

"Have you hear—" She starts to say.

"No." I interrupt her. "And I rather not think about him, it's bad enough as it is."

"I'm sorry, Sarah, but I just can't believe it." She says sadly. "Look I know this won't help, but let me just tell you that I really think he will call, you'll see." She smiles and takes a sip of her water.

"I doubt it, but I won't be waiting around, anyway." I say hoping she drops the subject.

When I get back to the office Marcia is on the phone behind her desk. When she sees me walking in she suddenly hangs up and pretends to be looking through the papers in front of her. I give her a peculiar look as I walk by her and see her flinch, something not very usual for her. Thinking of what she could be up to, my attention is broken by Larry who's walking down the hallway with a bunch of folders.

"Hey!" He smiles.

"Hi Larry." I say as I walk towards Amy's, er, my office.

"Um, Sara?" I hear him say behind me.

"Yes?" I answer as I turn to face him.

"I-I was wondering if…" He shifts the folders on his other arm, looks down and then back up again. "Would you like to go out, uh… sometime? Go out with me, to dinner or something?"

Okay… this is unexpected. "Well, I – sure, why not?" I hear myself saying. "That would be great."

"Okay, then." He says and turns to walk down the hallway.

I start to turn around myself, but stop and call after him. "Larry?" He turns slowly. "When would you want to go?"

"Oh!" He laughs sheepishly. "Sure, yes, that would help wouldn't it?

I nod.

"Let's see…" He says thoughtfully. "How about if we go somewhere right after work on, say, Thursday?"

"Sounds good." I smile and turn again towards Amy's - my office. My office. Did I just make a date with Larry? Hmm… well, I guess that's good, he's a nice guy. I need to get out and keep my mind off Biel. This is good, I think it will be nice to get to know Larry better.

Walking into my office I realize that now I go left in the hallway, instead of right to go to the closet, so I pass by Neil's old office. It's still empty. With two senior designers gone I would think that Mr. Tivoli would see to it that they be replaced. Oh well, whatever. Sitting down on my desk I think back to the run-in with Ivan at lunch. I almost laugh out loud thinking about it, I mean the nerve of him after what he did to try to get back together! I guess it shouldn't surprise me, really, after all he is an idiot who's full of himself.

When I tell Courtney that I'm going on a date with Larry she says it's great, but I can hear the disappointment in her voice. She really hoped that it would work with Biel and I and keeps insisting that he'll come around. We've been through this discussion already quite a few times so I just sit quietly on the kitchen counter as she starts cooking dinner. I'm glad she doesn't say anything more because it's hard enough to try and forget everything that happened in Spain.

"Need any help?" I ask her feeling a little useless as I sit watching her put some water to boil. She said she was making spaghetti with ground turkey and vegetables. Not waiting for her answer I get up and take out some frozen vegetables from the freezer.

"They can go for about four minutes in the micro." She says as she sees me looking at the bag for the instructions.

A while later we're eating our creation out in the balcony. It's a nice evening out, very mild with just a slight breeze and the ocean waves make for great background noise. As we eat dessert the phone rings and Courtney gets up to get it, since it's probably Santi. She comes back outside as she's saying good night to him and I'm taken aback when she says 'I love you' before hanging up.

I glance at her and grin.

"What?" She says and I can see her blush slightly. I shake my head smiling.

"So… how's Biel? Did he say?" I find myself asking before I can stop.

She smiles and takes a sip of water. "Well, he says he misses you, but he's not talking much these days."

"Oh well, whatever." I say frustrated at myself for bringing it up. "Going out with Larry will be good. He's a nice guy, I think we'll have a good time." Courtney shrugs and starts to clear the table. I take what's left on the table and follow her in.

"You and Santi seem to be getting serious…" I say as I put some glasses and silverware into the sink.

She smiles under her breath. "Yeah… things are good."

"I'm glad for you, really I mean it." I say as I look her in the eye. "I think it's great for you guys."

She sighs and puts her hand on my arm. "Thanks. And I really hoped it would've been the same… you know, for you. I'm really sorry."

"I know, me too."

When Thursday arrives, I find myself a little nervous. I run into Larry in the hall as I walk towards my office. He says hello awkwardly and I smile in return.

"Any thought as to where we could go eat later?" He asks, almost in one breath.

"Uh… I haven't really thought about it…" I say truthfully. I've been thinking about the date, but haven't put much thought as to where we could go. "But, anywhere is fine with me."

"Alright, I'll think of something." He smiles and winks before continuing down the hall.

When I get to my desk there are two messages taped to my phone. One says Mr. Tivoli would like to see me, the other to call Ivan. I take the second one and pitch it in the garbage as I shake my head. The one from Mr. Tivoli says he is expecting me at around eleven if that's okay. Looking back at the phone I see that the voicemail light is blinking. I hit the message button thinking to myself that I don't remember ever having so many messages in one shot.

"Sarah, call me. I want to take you to dinner this Saturday. I can't Friday, but on Saturday I'm free. So call. Please." Ivan's voice comes through the receiver. I laugh out loud as I hit the Delete button. What did I ever see in this guy?

Later I find myself sitting on Mr. Tivoli's couch drinking a coke.

"I'm sorry to bring you up here." He starts and takes a sip of his grape juice. "It's just that we think Neil took some files with him when he left." He pauses to look at me.

"Oh?" I say, not finding this very surprising.

"Apparently he's trying to get Mr. Halifax as his client." He walks over to the window. "He took copies of your designs and we think he's trying to convince him that they were his all along."

"What?" I say almost laughing.

"With the amount of work that Mr. Halifax wanted to contract for, he would provide enough income for the year for one person." Mr. Tivoli goes on as he sits back on the couch.

"But Mr. Halifax knows Neil didn't do those, he's not stupid." I say.

"I know, but that's not really the problem." He looks straight at me. "It seems that he took some confidential files also and is trying to bring us down."

"How?" This doesn't look good.

Mr. Tivoli sits back and sighs. "Well, he took some files, and now he's claiming that we're trying to use his designs after he was let go." He takes another sip of grape juice. "The designs he took were from your computer."

"My computer?" I can't believe that bastard.

"The other computers were all connected to a server that recorded all the files that were copied." He says. Apparently my computer's model was too old and not compatible with the server so anything could be copied with no record. He then erased them from my hard drive so they couldn't be traced to me.

"How did you find out about it?" I ask, curious.

"Mr. Halifax actually called." He says. "He recognized your designs, he said they looked like your work. He also knew Neil was fired and thought he was up to no good."

This Mr. Halifax doesn't stop surprising me, I can't believe he could recognize my style in the design files Neil took, they were completely different than the ones I did for his account.

"He also had a friend who is pretty good with computers analyze the files and he could tell they didn't originate from Neil's computer." Mr. Tivoli added as he poured more grape juice in his glass. "More coke?"

"No thanks, I'm good." I answer taking my last gulp. "Mr. Tivoli, will you be hiring any more designers?"

He turns from the mini refrigerator and sits back down on the couch. "Well, that's another thing I wanted to see you about." He starts as he leans back. "I've already talked to Larry about making him Senior Designer and he will hire someone to start as an Entry Level Designer."

"That's good." I don't see why he'd want to talk to me about it, but it's good for Larry, he deserves it. Maybe he'll ask if I want to take the position as the Entry Level Designer, which would be a nice change from being the Junior, that's for sure..

"Yes, it is." He says matter-of-factly. "But, I also wanted you to be a Senior member in the Art Department because you've shown yourself to be quite an asset. However, I don't want to put the pressure, so please think about it and let me know."

I'm silent for a few seconds as I put this in perspective. Wow! A Senior member! That's a huge step from the Entry Level position!! But, I mean, with Brian running the company I don't know what it will be like… "Okay… Can I think about it for a few days?"

"Yes, of course." He smiles. "Just not too long, I need to get that department running and back in order." He snickers.

Well, things are looking better. I just have to make up my mind about this job. I still like the idea of doing freelance, but maybe this could be good experience. It is also inevitable that my salary will go up, which is good and will ensure my rent for the beach apartment for many months to come.

All this and I still can't keep away the feeling of sadness to wash over once again when I think about Biel. How great it would be to tell him about all these news. Alright, Sara, stop it. I have a date with Larry tonight, I should concentrate on that. It will be fun. Everything will be okay and I'll forget about Biel.

But, what if I can't? What if I'll always feel this bad?

Twenty-nine

Since I don't have to do all the 'Junior' duties anymore, like turn everything off when everyone leaves, I'm done with work at about six. Now the last person to use something is the one that turns it off. All the other machines that we don't use or that are left on, are turned off by Marcia, which is the way it always was before Neil and Brian came up with the brilliant Junior position.

Larry is already waiting by the elevators when I come out to the reception area. I say hello as I walk up to him. He smiles shifting his weight. "Uh, I thought we could go to this place near here in Las Olas, Down's Grill, what do you think?"

"Sure! Sounds fine." The place sounds familiar, but then again so do half the places in Las Olas since I've either been to them, or went by them at some point.

The place is packed when we get there, so we put our name down on the waiting list. We take a walk down the sidewalk as we wait for the beeper they gave us to go off.

"I hear that you've been promoted." I say to him as we walk by a group dressed in office attire.

He smiles blushing a little. "Yes, I have." Then he looks at me sideways. "How about you? I hear you might also—" A loud beeping noise interrupts him and we realize it's the beeper going off.

"That was fast!" I say, glad that we didn't' have to wait too long.

Once we're seated I look around and see that every table is full. In a corner table I notice the group of office people we passed on the sidewalk.

"Here you go, Sara." I turn to see Larry handing me a menu. As I go to grab it he accidentally hits my glass of water with it.

I yelp as I quickly stand when the cold water splashes all over my skirt and legs.

"I'm so sorry!" He quickly comes around with a napkin.

"It's okay, I'm alright don't worry." I sit back down and laugh stupidly. The waiter also comes over with more napkins, handing me one and wiping the table with the others.

A while later, almost dry and with our food in front of us, we're interrupted by someone who comes up from somewhere behind me.

"Hello, Sara." I turn and see Ivan standing there grinning.

"Ivan." I murmur and look apologetically at Larry, who's looking a bit uncomfortable.

Ivan just stands there as if waiting for something. As the situation gets more uncomfortable I try to think of something to say so he'll leave.

"Uh, well, it's nice to see you Ivan." I smile hopefully at him. "I'm sure your date must be waiting."

"Who's your friend?" He asks smiling, although I can hear the tenseness in his voice.

I look at Larry who's seems very uneasy and is shifting in his chair. "This is Larry, we work together."

Ivan beams at him and offers his hand. "Nice to meet you, I'm Ivan, Sara's boyfriend."

Larry frowns as he takes Ivan's hand and shakes it.

"Ex-boyfriend." I say firmly looking at Larry.

"Oh, yeah, yeah, I meant ex-boyfriend." He smirks. "But, I'm working on the 'ex' part." He giggles. "I really want to work it out with Sara, I mean you guys are just friends, so I'm sure there's no problem."

Larry is really uneasy and I'm feeling quite weird myself with this whole scenario.

"Listen, Ivan, we'll talk later ok?" I tell him trying to smile like it's no big deal. "We're hungry and have to talk about some stuff."

"Sure, of course, sweets. I'll call you" He stands for a few seconds more smiling like an idiot and then he tramples back to his table. I feel like I should've been more firm and told him straight out to go to hell, but I didn't want to make a scene. I rather deal with him when there isn't an audience present.

"I'm so sorry." I say to Larry who's still shifting in his chair with a sour look on his face. "He's a little, you know, uh, unbalanced. I just wanted him to go away and he just can't take a hint!" I laugh nervously.

Except for a few comments about the latest developments at work, we don't say much for the rest of the dinner. In fact it's very tense and uncomfortable and neither of us orders dessert or coffee so we can just leave. When the bill finally arrives I'm sighing in relief inside.

"Shit." Larry says as he fidgets with his pant pocket.

"You okay?" I ask amused as he keeps touching his behind.

"Uh...." He giggles anxiously. "You won't believe this, but I forgot my wallet."

Larry parks his car in one of the guest spots and turns the engine off. Trying to pretend all is normal, I turn to him and say good night as I quickly get out of the car. I hope he's not counting on a kiss or anything, I wish he would've just dropped me off by the stairs without parking.

He also gets out of the car and starts to walk next to me.

"I'll walk you to your door." He smiles softly. "You know, make sure you make it in alright."

"Thanks." I say hoping he's not thinking of anything else. "It's pretty safe here, I mean you don't have to worry."

As we reach my door I turn to say goodnight. He puts his hands in his pockets and sighs.

"Listen, Sara, I know tonight was a disaster." He says nervously. "But I hope we can still be friends and not let this date make it uncomfortable every time we see each other."

Grateful that he sees things as I do, I smile and loosen up a little. "I'm sure we'll be laughing about tonight. I mean, you have to admit looking back at everything, it was kind of funny!"

He laughs. "It was quite memorable." He says, noticeably more relaxed now. "I also owe you one. I can't believe I left my wallet, I felt so stupid!"

"Don't worry, you'll get me next time." I say taking my keys out of my purse.

"Hey, I hope things work out with Ivan." He says sounding sincere. Before I know it I find myself spilling out the story about Ivan, Biel, Spain etc... and surprisingly he listens to the whole thing. This guy can really be a good friend.

He offers some advice and tells me to definitely stay away from Ivan and if I need any help in keeping him at a distance to let him know.

"I'm sorry about Biel." He tells me as he starts to leave. "Sometimes we're better off alone for a while, you know sometimes when you're not looking for anyone, that's when they appear." He laughs.

"Thanks, Larry." I smile as I get in the door and wave good bye to him. Somehow I get the feeling that's what he's doing. He might have thought I was the one that 'appeared'. Poor Larry, I'm sure someone will appear soon, he really is a nice guy.

On Saturday we go to the beach for an all day affair; it's nice to be with the girls again, since I hadn't seen them in a while. I'm surprised and for some reason a little bothered that Santi doesn't mention Biel. But I guess I should just get used to it, hard as it might be, I have to let go of that stupid hope that he could have a change of heart. I should take it as a clue that Courtney hasn't said much about him either.

"Hey, I heard about your night with Larry, wow, what a disaster!" Lydia says when we walk to the water for a swim. I half smile at her without answering.

"Do you think he'd consider a date with moi?" She winks and dives into the waves. Everyone else follows into the water and for the first time in a while I find myself having a good time. We brought a bunch of food so we have a huge lunch under our umbrellas, it's really cozy and the soft breeze feels great.

The rest of the day turns out to be great, we eat, play volleyball, swim, talk and eat some more. It's not until some time later in the evening when I find myself sitting alone in the balcony staring out to the sea that Biel's name pops itself into my mind again. Memories of my trip to Spain flood back and seeing Courtney and Santi laughing on the couch together as they watch a movie, just makes me even more nostalgic. I sigh and look back out to the ocean, telling myself that I'll be alright. As hard as that is to believe right now, eventually things will be better.

Next Monday I'm greeted by a surprise visit from Mr. Halifax. He has finalized all the designs and they go to the printer next Thursday. Now he's here because he wants another brochure for something new. He gives me all the preliminaries and tells me to be creative and do whatever I think is best.

For the next few days I immerse myself with my new project and hardly have time for anything else. This is great because it gives me the opportunity to forget about all the dilemmas that I don't want to think about. I even stay late doing two and three different designs of everything.

"This looks really great!" Courtney says one night as I lay all my stuff out on the couch to get a look at what I have so far. "I'm glad things worked out for you at your job." She says as we remember how ridiculous it got to be with Neil and Amy.

"I think I'll even be going to the next Design Conference too." I say, remembering the trip to St. Croix with Biel and Santi. Courtney says that Santi will be going also and he invited her to go.

Thinking into this I realize something. "You know, Larry is going too, how about if we ask Lydia to come?"

"Why not? I think it could work, she keeps asking you about him since that day at the beach."

I wonder where this one is going to be, they haven't disclosed the location yet because they said the committee couldn't agree on a place. It will be nice to get away for a while, even if everyone around me will be coupled off.

I spend the next few days doing more designs and just taking time off on the weekend to go to the beach. The conference trip is not for another 2 weeks so I have plenty of time to present Mr.

Halifax with something before I go. Actually, I'll have tons of stuff for him, I'm on a roll with this and can't stop spewing different designs out.

On Tuesday evening I'm starting to feel the effects of my non-stop design spree. I leave the office at five thirty and decide that it's time for a little break. I'll go home order pizza and watch a movie. Courtney and Biel are going out tonight so I'll have the place to myself. Incidentally, Larry and Lydia are also going out tonight; I set them up and both seem quite up for the date. As I make my way out I tell Larry good bye and to have a good time.

As I go up the stairs to the apartment I notice someone sitting at the top stair. It's pretty dark and I can't make out the familiar silhouette, I go up a few stairs and freeze mid-step.

"Hi Sara."

My heart stops for a second as I find myself looking into Biel's face. He looks kind of miserable and sad.

"Hi…" I hardly know what to say. "How come… you're here, Biel?"

He stands and takes a couple of steps down to face me.

"Sara… I…" He shakes his head and looks down. "I'm an idiot. I'm a real stupid idiot. And I am so sorry." He looks back up and touches my cheek but quickly puts his hand down again.

I just stand there speechless, feeling quite like the idiot myself. I want to say something, but nothing comes out.

"Look, I understand if you just send me to hell, but I want to apologize for being a coward to you." He stops and takes my hand. "I've been miserable since I saw you the last time. I thought I would get over you and be able to be by myself for a while."

I just wait for him to keep talking.

"I want to be with you Sara, you're more than worth the risk of getting hurt again."

Still speechless, I sit down on the steps. Biel sits down next to me.

"Sara?" He says trying to look at my face. "I just want you to please give me another chance."

I look back at him, still not saying anything. He starts to get up.

"Please think about it, okay? Just think about it." He stands there a few seconds before starting to make his way down the steps.

"Biel?" I stand up and grab his hand. He turns around and we just stand there. Out of nowhere, I throw my arms around him and hug him, he pulls me closer and I feel tears in my eyes.

"I've missed you.' I finally manage to say. "I've missed you so much."

"I'm sorry." He wipes my eyes and pulls my face to his and kisses me. I don't know how long we stand there hugging and kissing, but when we finally pull apart he pulls a picture from his pocket and hands it to me.

"It's my beach!" I say looking at the picture of the beach he and Santi named after me. There's an official looking sign that says 'Sara's Beach' posted on the sand. "How did you get the sign there?"

He winks. "I have connections…"

"I wish we could go back there again." I say as I imagine us swimming in the crystal clear water.

"You are going back." He says smiling.

"I don't have any vacation time until next year.' I say disillusioned.

"You are going before that." He says with a mischievous half smile. "Guess where the Advertising Convention is going to be?"

"But I thought they didn't have a place…"

"Now they do. They picked it again because everyone liked it there so much." He says, not very convincingly. I stare at him skeptically.

"Are you sure that's why?" I tease.

"And… I happen to know some of the people at the organizing committee." He laughs.

"You just now everyone, don't you?" He smiles and kisses me again.

I take his hand and we go towards the apartment. As I open the door he pulls me to him again, he leans his forehead onto mine. "We have to make up for all the time we lost." We kiss once more and then I realize that I'm starving.

"Ok… let's start with some food!" I take him to the kitchen and get some bread and tomatoes out. "I've been dying for some of that tomato bread you make." As he gets to work on our dinner, I go to my room and get something I bought for him in

Spain. I go back to the kitchen and give him a little stuffed whale. The one he always wanted as a child, but his mom could never find.

"Here." I say holding it out to him. He stares at it and then smiles as he gently takes it from my hand.

His eyes twinkle as he looks at the little whale and then at me.

"Thank you." He pulls me to him and hugs me tightly. "I love you, Sara."

THE END